8·7·73

8·7·73

The Elizabethan Theatre III

The Elizabethan Theatre III

Papers given at the Third International
Conference on Elizabethan Theatre held at the
University of Waterloo, Ontario, in July 1970

Edited and with an introduction by
DAVID GALLOWAY
Department of English
University of New Brunswick

Published in collaboration with the
University of Waterloo

Archon Books

© 1973 by the Macmillan Company of Canada Limited

Published in Canada by the Macmillan Company of Canada Limited and
simultaneously published in the United States of America as an Archon Book
by The Shoestring Press, Inc., Hamden, Connecticut.

Library of Congress Catalog Card No. 72-88875

Library of Congress Cataloging in Publication Data

International Conference on Elizabethan Theatre, 3d,
University of Waterloo, 1970. The Elizabethan theatre III.

Includes bibliographical references.
1. Shakespeare, William, 1564-1616—Stage history—to 1625—Congresses.
2. Theatre—England—History—Congresses. I. Galloway, David D., ed. II.
Waterloo, Ont. University. III. Title.
PR3095.15 1970   792'.0942   72-13465
ISBN 0-208-01331-8

Acknowledgments

In acknowledging the help which I have received in organizing the Third International Conference on Elizabethan Theatre and in editing this book which grew out of it, I thank several people who have loyally supported me for the third year running, and say to them, with Thaisa in *Pericles*, "Your recompense is thanks, that's all. Yet my good will is great."

Once more the conference was made possible by the financial support of the Canada Council and the University of Waterloo. As usual, H. E. Petch, Academic Vice-President, gave much support but asked few questions, and I can only hope that the results justified his trust. It is not easy to arrange conferences by remote control and, while in New Brunswick, I was much relieved to know that so much of the organization was in the capable hands of David Hedges, the Assistant Director and man on the spot. Shirley Thomson, once again, and Laura Owen were in charge of registration; Carol Jerusalem, Betty McCutchan (now Breithaupt), Lee Owen, Edith Rice and Beryl Reeves all showed a willingness to help which went far beyond mundane commitments; and, thanks to the hospitality of the University of Waterloo Faculty Club, the conference could "drink to th' general joy o' th' whole table." I should like to thank D. F. Rowan for reading Glynne Wickham's paper in Professor Wickham's absence, and Evelyn Gair for preparing the index for this book.

For the third time I am grateful to the Macmillan Company of Canada for publishing these papers, and especially to Pat Meany and to Diane Mew, the Executive Editor, College Division, who, in spite of a number of delays, usually of my own causing, bore all with patience and enduring good humour.

D.G.

Contents

Introduction

It was intended that the theme of this volume, the papers given at the Third International Conference on Elizabethan Theatre, held at the University of Waterloo in July 1970, should be "The Theatre and Society," and a cynic might argue that such a topic covers any eventuality. Editors of conference papers, however, are sometimes amazed to find, after reading the papers as a whole, that emphases which were originally intended do not make the impact planned, and other emphases emerge. In various ways four papers—those of Clifford Leech, Glynne Wickham, W. R. Gair and George R. Kernodle—do show society as having a direct impact on the content of the plays which they discuss; but a second theme, perhaps not quite so strongly, comes to the fore—a concern with the structure of the theatre in which actor and playwright worked. *Elizabethan Theatre* [I] was largely concerned with the structure of certain Elizabethan theatres; *Elizabethan Theatre II* to some extent continued the story with stress on the dramatic companies and their personnel; *Elizabethan Theatre III* shows a reluctance to let the subject drop, especially in the papers of T. J. King, Clifford Leech, Herbert Berry and J. A. Lavin.

In the first paper, T. J. King gives an informal report on the findings of his book, *Shakespearean Staging, 1599-1642* (Cambridge, Mass., 1971), "which offers a systematic survey of the staging requirements for 276 plays first performed by professionals between the autumn of 1599, when Shakespeare's company probably first acted at the Globe, and 1642, when the theatres were closed by order of Parliament" (p. 1). Professor King tries to "establish positive correlations" between pictorial and architectural evidence and evidence provided by the texts of the plays themselves, and he discusses the "generally accepted evidence available" about the stage of the period—the De Witt sketch of the Swan; the hall screens at Hampton Court and the Middle Temple; Inigo Jones's drawings for the remodelled

Cockpit-in-Court and the drawings for an un-identified pre-Restoration playhouse, both of them in the Jones/Webb collection at Worcester College, Oxford; a scale drawing of Trinity Hall, Aldersgate, London; the *Roxana* and *Messalina* title pages, and the *Wits* frontispiece. He points out that the nine façades are of two basic designs—either doorways and an open space above or a gallery from which curtains can be hung—and that either of these designs can, "with minor adjustments, provide a suitable façade in front of which to act all of the texts that may depend on prompt copy from an English professional company in the years 1599-1642" (p. 4).

The nucleus of Professor King's textual evidence for his study is "the eighteen extant playhouse documents, including prompt-books, manuscripts dependent on playhouse copy, and printed plays with manuscript prompter's markings, for plays first performed by professionals in the period between late 1599 and 1642" (p. 5). After offering an imposing display of data, he concludes that "there were no significant differences in the staging requirements of the various companies and that the stage equipment needed was much simpler than has been thought" (p. 8); that machinery was not required in the large majority of plays; that "the basic requirement for the performance of Shakespeare's plays is an unlocalized façade through which actors can enter and large properties can be *brought on* or *thrust out*" (p. 13); and that actors readily improvised according to the stage facilities available to them.

Professor King ends with the hope that his study will "extend the structure of valid inference," "limit the field of admissible conjecture," free Shakespeare's readers from the misconception that his plays were acted in settings such as "a street" or "a room at the castle," and encourage modern producers "to follow this simple, flexible mode of production" (p. 13).

At first sight the title of the second paper, Clifford Leech's "Three Times *Ho* and a Brace of Widows: Some Plays for the Private Theatre," might suggest an opinion differing with Professor King's statement that "there were no significant differences in the staging requirements of the various companies." Professor Leech, however, suggests no firm dichotomy between "public" and "private," although he does see the three *Ho* plays as having been written for an in-group "whose members rivalled each other, could· even show respect for each other as well as an occasional mockery, could make in-jokes which its audience could be expected to take up" (p. 15). The society which attended these plays also went to the public theatres but "the reverse cannot have been wholly true. At Paul's and the Blackfriars you could have a sense of being at the club: the *profanum vulgus* was without, and could be safely mocked" (p. 15). Professor Leech's study of the *Ho* plays suggests links between them in date of composition, in staging, in style, in the objects of their satire, and in their being "plays within plays" with numerous quotations from, and parodies and echoes of, other plays of the period. *Northward Ho*, however, is a disappointment, with "neither the sentimental complexity of *Westward Ho* nor the astringent burlesque of *Eastward Ho*" (p. 27). In spite of the *Ho* plays being for the private theatre, however, Professor Leech's conclusions are complementary rather than opposed to Professor King's, for the differences between these plays for the private theatre and others more obviously suitable for the public theatre lie in their literary content and in their attitudes to society rather than in any peculiar demands of their staging.

Herbert Berry, in "The Boar's Head Again," returns to a discussion of the playhouse in Whitechapel about which he wrote in detail in *Elizabethan Theatre* [I], where, mainly from a tangle of lawsuits, dating from 1599-1603, he produced a clearer, if still somewhat tentative, structural picture than we had had before. Now, in the second part of his work, Professor Berry explains "some events leading up to the lawsuits," discusses "some of the people concerned in them," and explains "more closely than I could two years ago what the yard of the Boar's Head may have looked like and what happened to it in the years from then until now" (p. 33). After discussing the adventures of the Poleys, Woodliffes, Samwell, Browne, Langley and others familiar to us from the pages of part one, and after scrutinizing various maps of the seventeenth, eighteenth and nineteenth centuries, Professor Berry is able to conclude that, by December 1621, "the Boar's Head playhouse was no more, and the Boar's Head itself was rapidly becoming a tangle of small holdings, an enclave off Whitechapel" (p. 42). He is able to make "some shrewd guesses about what the Boar's Head was like before the building of the playhouse in 1598 and 1599" (p. 52), he can be "surer of what much of the playhouse looked like," and he can be "nearly positive of some of the important ways in which the inn changed later" (p.

53). Professor Berry deduces the dimensions of the stage, yard and galleries, reproduces a scale plan and, finally, in pointing out the site, advises the Greater London Council where it can put its blue plaque.

In "Shakespeare and the Second Blackfriars," J. A. Lavin, with his usual vigour, attacks the carelessness "endemic in every area of literary scholarship" (p. 66), and especially "the notion that the physical characteristics of a particular theatre determined or heavily affected the literary features of the plays" (p. 67). Attacking particularly the view that "the acquisition of the Blackfriars Theatre by the King's Men in 1609 brought about a complete change in Shakespeare's methods and style" (p. 68), he directs most of his strictures at G. E. Bentley, an arch-exponent of such a view in *Shakespeare and his Theatre* (1964). He deals with several of Professor Bentley's arguments in detail, and shows how "through the cumulative effect of repetition, conjecture is established as fact" (p. 78). Professor Lavin asserts "categorically that there is not a shred of evidence to show that the dramaturgy of Elizabethan playwrights was materially affected by the physical arrangements of the public playhouses, and that in fact all the available evidence points in the opposite direction" (p. 78). He concludes by urging us not to forget that, although Shakespeare's plays were written under pressure and for money, "he was also a self-conscious artist, craftsman, and poet" (p. 81).

Glynne Wickham, in "Romance and Emblem: A Study in the Dramatic Structure of *The Winter's Tale*," notes the apparent paradox that the drama of those ill-assorted bedfellows, England and Spain, "during the closing decades of the sixteenth century has gained the lasting respect of posterity, while no such phenomenon occurred in other countries at that time" (p. 82). He suggests that "a partial answer is to be found once it is realized that in these two countries alone the gothic tradition of typological, prefigurative and emblematic methods of play construction survived virtually intact, absorbing en route such new ideas common to the age as were useful" (p. 83). By contrast, the courtly societies of Italy and France turned their backs on the gothic past "and entered eagerly upon a phase of academic antiquarianism in playwriting and theatrical representation" (p. 83). In England and Spain, with less support—or interference—from court and academic patrons, the theatre became more profes-

sional in the hands of actor-playwright-director managers such
as Shakespeare and Jonson, Lope de Vega and Calderón, and the
emblematic play, "better suited than any other to professional
actors trafficking between palace and public playhouse . . . enabled
them to discuss religious, political, and social issues notwithstanding the censorship" (p. 84).

Professor Wickham sees *The Winter's Tale* as an emblematic
play, rooted in Anglo-Scottish relations of the sixteenth century,
representing an attempt to heal old wounds after the Gunpowder
Plot "by recourse to mercy, forgiveness, and regenerative love,"
and, more specifically, representing "Shakespeare's contribution
to the celebrations marking the investiture of Henry Stuart as
Prince of Wales and heir apparent to the reunited Kingdoms of
England, Wales and Scotland in June 1610" (p. 88). He draws his
main supporting evidence from Rubens' depiction of the reuni-
fication of the kingdom on the ceiling of the Banqueting House at
Whitehall, from Anthony Munday's Lord Mayor's Pageants, *The
Triumphs of a re-united Britania* (1605), from Samuel Daniel's *A
Panegyricke Congratulatory* (1603), from the court masque,
Tethys Festival, by Daniel and Inigo Jones, and from Arthur
Wilson's *History of Great Britain under James I.* For Professor
Wickham, the basis of the emblematic structure—with the
sixteen-year time-gap as an essential component—is "Union and
Harmony, followed by Divorce, Disintegration or Discord, followed by Reunion and future happiness with Time, Faith and
the fulfilment of prophecy as the translating agents" (p. 97).
Indeed, "we have in *The Winter's Tale* a work of art directly comparable with Rubens' idealization of the Union. . . . Political
didactism informs composition and construction in picture and
play respectively; but such is the mastery of style and technique
that in each case the diagrammatic moralizing of the moment is
transcended by the enduring artistry of the entire work. Yet the
structure of the work remains rooted in the events it celebrates"
(p. 99).

Like Professor Wickham, W. R. Gair, in "The Politics of
Scholarship: A Dramatic Comment on the Autocracy of Charles
I," is concerned with the importance of a political event to a
specific play, but in a more direct, more literal and less far-
reaching manner. Dr. Gair's society is that of the antiquaries
although, as he points out, the work of the antiquary could be
used as a political weapon and had, for example, "a direct

relevance to the struggle between Parliament and Crown" (p. 113). He begins with the central incident in the main plot of Shackerly Marmion's *The Antiquary*, which "occurs when Veterano, the antiquarian of the title," hears that "the duke has been informed of your rarieties" and "hath sent his mandamus to take them from you" (p. 100). Dr. Gair sees this incident as having had "a powerful emotive effect upon the contemporary audience"—an effect which "can best be understood by us in terms of the history of the Elizabethan Society of Antiquaries" (p. 100). In his sketch of the history of the Society, he discusses the importance of Archbishop Parker, Leyland, Bale, Camden, Dee, Lambarde and others, shows how the preservation of manuscripts was bound up with national feelings, and how the Privy Council used the Society for political purposes. The central incident of *The Antiquary*, in fact, is a dramatic comment on Sir Robert Cotton's arrest and the closure of his library in 1629. Marmion's play, however, "consistently allows the antiquary to state his case and to argue that his profession is one worthy of admiration" (p. 116), and represents an adverse comment on the autocratic behaviour of Charles I and his Privy Council.

In a wide-ranging paper, "The Mannerist Stage of Comic Detachment," George R. Kernodle expresses his gratitude to the art historians for wedging another period, the Mannerist, between the Renaissance and the Baroque. The change from Renaissance to Mannerist is dramatized pictorially in the two great paintings of Michelangelo in the Sistine Chapel. The painting on the ceiling, extremely complex, but subordinated to the overall effect of order and control, is in marked contrast with the Last Judgment, in which "there is no firm structure" and "the overall impression is one of tortured complexity" (p. 121). In the theatre, the Italian perspective settings of the early and mid sixteenth century give way to light, painted changeable forms, moveable scenery, cloud machines, and all the stage magic which seems to express "the new restlessness and sense of change of the Mannerist age" (p. 122)—an age summed up in Donne's phrase "all coherence gone."

The beginning of the seventeenth century, typified by *Hamlet* and *King Lear* in England, sees one of the great crises of ·the human soul. "The major change was a separation of man from nature, a change that required not only new philosophical concepts but new ways of feeling" (p. 122). Out of this crisis, says

Professor Kernodle, both science and high comedy were born, and he follows this "bifurcation of the mind" into the four great tragedies of Shakespeare, into the world of Bacon and Galileo and others who set out "to dry up the ocean of subjective feeling," into the *commedia dell'arte*, and into the comedies of Ben Jonson, Molière, Etherege, Congreve and Sheridan. Professor Kernodle finds, in the work of Strindberg, Pirandello and O'Neill, "the same restless skepticism that we see in the earlier Mannerist age," and he discusses the theatre of the absurd as an expression of protest and rebellion. "Signs of new definitions of comic detachment similar to those in the old Mannerist age" appear in films such as *La Dolce Vita* and *Blow-Up*, and in plays such as *Marat/Sade*, *Who's Afraid of Virginia Woolf* and *Rosencrantz and Guildenstern are Dead*. "When we realize how long it was from the bitter comedy of Ben Jonson to the more urbane disillusionment of Molière and to the brisk, witty players of games in Congreve and Sheridan, we can hope that our Mannerist age of confusion, disillusion, and pain has made a start towards a new high comedy —a new way of watching the world and also being part of it" (p. 134).

In the final paper, "Continuity and Innovation in Shakespeare's Art," John Lawlor is not concerned with the manner in which theatre and society influence one another directly, nor is he concerned with the physical structure of the playhouse. He is, however, deeply concerned with "Shakespeare's theatrecraft, those skills and resources which are characteristic of Shakespeare the working dramatist" (p. 135). Professor Lawlor asks the "hard but inevitable question—what is the veritably Shakespearian? How can we hope to get at that which is central in each play?" (p. 136). He discusses the dangers in "approaches" to Shakespeare, and the dangers of seeing a "contemporary" Shakespeare, an "Elizabethan" Shakespeare, or, even, a "timeless" Shakespeare, with criticism obstinately projecting on the work "its own preconceptions, including images of the writer himself" (p. 138). In seeking the "veritably Shakespearian" Professor Lawlor asks us "at every stage" to "remind ourselves of the width of Shakespeare's production," to "scrutinize all instances within any one play of the business or definitive gesture that invests a major scene," and to seek the tension between poetry and history. Lear's reunion with Cordelia (IV.vii), and Hal's stooping to the Lord Chief Justice in *II Henry IV* (V.ii) and its prelude in *I*

Henry IV (II.iv) when Hal defers to Falstaff-as-King, are three of the scenes with which Professor Lawlor illustrates how "Shakespearian drama sustains a current of demonstrative energy, a pattern of action that draws upon the deepest yet most ordinary sense of what we may properly call "ritual," the means by which human beings assure themselves as well as others of their deepest intents. Recognition of this, and its effective re-enactment upon the stage, must prevent Shakespeare's work from ever being mistaken for merely a drama of ideas" p. 142).

In spite of the obvious variety of the papers, this volume—with its two predecessors—shows an explicit and implicit consciousness that Shakespeare and his fellow dramatists were men of the theatre, but not in the patronizing, finger-wagging manner in which professional actors and directors so often, and quite unnecessarily, remind "remote and ineffectual" dons who sometimes dare to attack their productions. Insistently, in the three volumes of *Elizabethan Theatre*, in fact, in spite of some false starts and essays into *cul-de-sacs*, there has been a probing to find out how the plays actually worked on the stage. As we have seen, the idea that playwrights wrote with specific theatres narrowly in mind has been grossly overstressed, and Professors King and Lavin give support to Professor Wickham's statements in *Elizabethan Theatre* [I] that playing conditions at court and in the public theatres were similar. However, although the same plays could be performed, with no more than minor adjustments, at court, at the Globe, at the Blackfriars, in the Inns of Court and in provincial guildhalls, Professor Leech reminds us that society, in the form of the audience, can sometimes determine the tone of a play. Dr. Gair gives an example of how a specific event can be used dramatically, and Professor Kernodle reminds us of how the drama can express the despair or the aspirations of a whole era. Structurally, the specific theatres of the Elizabethan period can now be seen to have been much more part of a general architectural *milieu* than we thought a few years ago. We used to smile, however, at the naïveté of scholars in the past who talked about "*the* Elizabethan Theatre," as though all theatres were the same. Today it might be salutary to remember that they were wiser than they knew.

David Galloway
Department of English
University of New Brunswick

The Elizabethan Theatre I I I

Shakespearian Staging,

1599-1642

T. J. KING

This is an informal report on the findings of my book, which offers a systematic survey of the staging requirements for 276 plays first performed by professionals between the autumn of 1599, when Shakespeare's company probably first acted at the Globe, and 1642, when the theatres were closed by order of Parliament.[1] My study does not offer a hypothetical reconstruction of a typical Elizabethan playhouse. Instead, I try to establish positive correlations between the available pictorial and architectural evidence concerning the English pre-Restoration stage and the evidence provided by the texts of the plays, especially the extant promptbooks and other playhouse documents that give authentic information about the way in which these plays were actually performed.

The pictorial and architectural evidence listed below has not been selected to support a priori assumptions of mine. Instead, it is all the generally accepted evidence available concerning the English stage of the period:

(1) The so-called De Witt sketch of the Swan, which is in fact Arend Van Buchell's pen-and-ink copy of De Witt's original, c. 1596. This structure was still standing in 1632. Sir Edmund Chambers points out that this is "our one contemporary picture of the interior of a public playhouse, and it is a dangerous business to explain away its evidence by an assumption of inaccurate observation on the part of De Witt, merely because that evidence

[1] Reprinted in part, by permission of the publishers, from T. J. King, *Shakespearean Staging, 1599-1642* (Cambridge, Mass.), 1971; © 1971 by the President and Fellows of Harvard College.

conflicts with subjective interpretations of stage-directions, arrived at in the course of the pursuit of a 'typical' stage."[2] The drawing shows a non-representational façade with two double-hung doors and a gallery above, where actors, or audience, or both, are observing action on stage.

(2) The hall screen at Hampton Court, built in 1531-1536, where the King's Men acted *Othello* on December 8, 1636, and *Hamlet* on January 24, 1636/7. The screen has two open doorways and a gallery above.

(3) The hall screen at the Middle Temple, originally built in 1574, damaged by enemy action during World War II, and reconstructed exactly according to the original design. *Twelfth Night* was acted here on February 2, 1601/2. The screen is a placeless façade with two doorways and a gallery above. Movable doors were added in 1671.[3]

(4) Inigo Jones's drawings for the remodelled Cockpit-in-Court at Whitehall. These form part of the so-called Jones/Webb Collection at Worcester College Library, Oxford. The renovated building was first used by the King's Men on November 5, 1630, when they offered "An Induction for the House," and Fletcher's play *The Mad Lover*. Court records for 1638 indicate that among the plays performed here were "Ceaser" on November 13, and "The mery wifes of winsor" on November 15. The drawing shows a placeless façade with five open entrance ways and an observation post above.[4]

(5) Drawings for an unidentified pre-Restoration playhouse also found in the Jones/Webb Collection, Worcester College Library. This stage has an unlocalized façade with three entrances and an observation post above.[5]

(6) A scale drawing of Trinity Hall, Aldersgate Street, London, reproduced by Charles T. Prouty. The drawing is dated 1782 when the hall was in use as a nonconformist chapel, but Prouty

[2] *The Elizabethan Stage*, III (Oxford, 1923), 526. Chambers reproduces this drawing on p. 521.

[3] Photographs of the hall screens at Hampton Court and at the Middle Temple are reproduced by Richard Hosley, "The Origins of the Shakespearian Playhouse," in *Shakespeare 400*, ed. James G. McManaway (New York, 1964), pp. 29-39.

[4] G. E. Bentley, *The Jacobean and Caroline Stage*, VI (Oxford, 1968), 267-284. The drawings follow page 276.

[5] These drawings were first published by D. F. Rowan, "A Neglected Jones/Webb Theatre Project: Barber-Surgeons Hall Writ Large," *New Theatre Magazine*, IX, No. 3 (Summer, 1969), 6-15.

maintains that it must have been built before 1446. Accounts of the Churchwardens of St. Botolph without Aldersgate show receipts from the rental of Trinity Hall to "diverse players" or "for playes" in seven of the years between 1557 and 1567. Prouty suggests that a curtain or arras was hung from the lower edge of the gallery at the western end of the hall, thus providing a tiring house or space within.[6] This curtain gives an unlocalized façade through which actors may enter by parting the curtain at either end or at the centre. The gallery above provides an observation post.

(7) A small engraving of a stage with actors on it from the title page of *Roxana*, 1632, a Latin play by William Alabaster, probably performed at Trinity College Cambridge, c. 1592. The play was first printed in London, however, about forty years after production and the engraving may therefore furnish evidence about the professional theatre at the time of printing. Curtains are hung from the downstage edge of the gallery above, from which actors, or audience, or both, are watching actors on stage.[7]

(8) A small engraving of a stage from the title page of *Messalina*, 1640, by Nathanael Richards. The play was probably acted by the King's Revels company sometime between July 1634 and May 1636, during which time the company was acting at Salisbury Court. Curtains are hung from what appears to be a gallery with a curtained window above.

(9) The frontispiece of *The Wits or Sport Upon Sport*, 1662, a collection of drolls probably acted in the Commonwealth or early Restoration periods. On stage are Falstaff, "The Changeling," and other characters from pre-Restoration plays. A curtain is hung from a gallery with a curtained window above. Actors, or audience, or both, are in the gallery watching actors on the stage below, where an actor is seen stepping from between the hangings.

Nicholas Rowe's edition of Shakespeare (1709) began the practice, followed by most subsequent editors, of adding designations of locale to the stage directions at the start of every scene, but these sophistications have no authority. Furthermore, Shakespeare's scenes are seldom precisely localized by the dialogue. In this connection it is important to note that the nine façades of

---

[6] "An Early Elizabethan Playhouse," *Shakespeare Survey 6* (1953), 64-74.
[7] C. Walter Hodges, *The Globe Restored* (London, 1953), reproduces *The Wits* drawing, p. 39, the *Messalina* drawing, Plate 44, and the *Roxana* drawing, Plate 45.

pre-Restoration stages listed here share the significant characteristic of being placeless. None of them represents a specific locale, as do the drawings of the tragic, comic, and pastoral settings for the Italian stage in Serlio's *Architettura* (1551).[8] Shakespeare and most other English dramatists of this period follow the convention that for some scenes a non-representational stage may gain temporary localization by a dialogue reference or by functional properties, such as a bed or a banquet, but when the stage is cleared of actors and properties, any designation of place that may have been suggested by the preceding scene is automatically nullified.

As we have seen, the nine stage façades are of two basic designs: (1) to (5) have doorways and an open space above; (6) to (9) have a gallery above from which curtains can be hung. Either of these basic designs can, with minor adjustments, provide a suitable façade in front of which to act all of the texts that may depend on prompt copy from an English professional company in the years 1599-1642. If a play requires hangings and is to be acted in a hall with doorways and a bare façade, hangings can be fitted over one or more of the doorways, perhaps for special scenes only. Evidence for this procedure is found in Philip Massinger's *The City Madam*, a King's Men play first acted in 1632 and printed with variant title pages, some dated 1658, others 1659. This text was apparently printed from prompt copy. Notations appear in the margins of the printed text just as they appear in the margins of some playhouse documents: *Whil'st the Act Plays, the Footstep, little Table, and Arras hung up for the Musicians* (IV.iv) and *Musicians come down to make ready for the song at Aras* (V.i).

No door frames are shown in the stage façades of the Trinity Hall, *Roxana, Messalina*, and *Wits* drawings, but a "door" in the sense of "a passage into a building or room; a doorway," can be provided by parting the hangings at the centre opening or at either end. One stage direction suggests that a movable door can be represented figuratively and need not be a literal part of the stage setting. James Shirley's *Love's Cruelty* (Q1, 1640)—licensed for the Queen's Men in 1631 and protected for Beeston's boys (young successors to the Queen's Men) in 1639—carries the direction *Hippolito seemes to open a chamber doore and brings forth Eubella* (IV).

In evaluating textual evidence I have tried to answer as fully as

[8] These drawings are reproduced by Chambers, IV, 259-362.

possible two important questions about each play: first, what historical evidence is there concerning the place and date of performance of this play by professional actors in the years 1599-1642; and second, what evidence is there to suggest that this text reflects the manner in which it was actually performed? In other words, how close to prompt copy is the manuscript or printed text that survives? The answers to these questions are hardly ever so certain as we could wish, but these are the first questions we should ask if we are to find valid textual evidence.

Although the preservation of early performance records is largely a matter of historical accident, it is clear that in these years Shakespeare's plays were acted not only at the first and second Globe but also at a minimum of six other places in the London area: Blackfriars, the Middle Temple, Whitehall, St. James, Hampton Court, and the Cockpit-in-Court. For Shakespeare's company—first known as the Lord Chamberlain's Men, which in 1603 became the King's Men—court performances were prestigious and lucrative engagements, especially in the reign of James I. It therefore seems likely that when Shakespeare wrote his plays, he had in mind not only the Globe but also the several royal entertainment halls. Other companies also acted at these court halls and at some of the same provincial towns where Shakespeare's company acted on its frequent tours.[9]

The nucleus of the textual evidence for this study is the eighteen extant playhouse documents, including prompt-books, manuscripts dependent on playhouse copy, and printed plays with manuscript prompter's markings, for plays first performed by professionals in the period between late 1599 and 1642. The significance of such documents is stressed by Sir Walter Greg:

> But though it is desirable to point out the caution needed in arguing from a restricted number of extant documents, it would be a serious error not to recognize their great importance for criticism. Every item of historical evidence performs a two-fold function: positively it enlarges the basis we have to build on, and enables us to extend the structure of valid inference; negatively it is often of even greater service in limiting the field of admissible conjecture. That is why to a certain type of mind all fresh evidence is so extremely distasteful. In the present case, when we have made reasonable allowance for indi-

[9] See Chambers, *William Shakespeare*, II (Oxford, 1930), 322-345 and Bentley, I (1941), 92-93.

vidual variation, the documents we are considering afford a very considerable and very valuable body of evidence.[10]

The stage directions in these playhouse documents not only provide authentic information concerning actual performance procedures but also serve as touchstones by which to form hypotheses about the extent to which a given text may depend on playhouse copy. Although scholars attempting to determine the substantive text of a play usually regard playhouse emendations as nonauthorial corruptions, these markings are a valuable source of evidence for the stage historian. I therefore give priority to the available prompt or theatrical versions, even though in some cases the non-theatrical texts of these plays may have greater authority. In general, the scholars I cite concerning the probable source of printer's copy for a given play accept the criteria established by R. B. McKerrow for inferring playhouse provenance of a text.[11] In general, these are warnings or anticipatory markings made by the prompter as reminders to have actors or properties in readiness before they are needed on stage, a practice followed by stage managers of the present day.

The significance of playhouse copy for the study of staging is illustrated by R. C. Bald, who offers a collation of two variant texts of John Fletcher's *The Woman's Prize,* a King's Men play first acted about 1611, and revived in 1633.[12] According to Bald, the manuscript of the play in the Lambarde Collection of the Folger Shakespeare Library gives a transcript of the prompt-book as the play was acted before 1623 when Sir Henry Herbert became Master of the Revels. A second version is printed in the Beaumont and Fletcher Folio of 1647 and is probably closer to the author's original text. Bald notes important differences in the stage directions. For example, where the Folio reads *Enter Livia discovered abed, and Moroso by her,* the manuscript reads "Enter Livia sick carryed in a chair by servants. Moroso by her." Bald suggests that, as originally written, production as indicated in the Folio was contemplated, though at some later date the exigencies of the theatre compelled an alteration. These changes are reflected in the manuscript.

[10] *Dramatic Documents from the Elizabethan Playhouses,* I (Oxford, 1931), x-xi.
[11] "The Elizabethan Printer and Dramatic Manuscripts," *The Library,* 4th Ser., XII (1931), 253-275.
[12] *Bibliographical Studies in the Beaumont & Fletcher Folio of 1647, Supplement to the Bibliographical Society's Transactions,* No. 13, 1938 (for 1937), pp. 77-78.

If Bald's inferences concerning the provenance of these texts are correct, then here is an example of how an acting company would improvise procedures according to the auditorium and stage properties available to them. This evidence also indicates that the stage equipment needed for pre-Restoration plays was not so elaborate or standardized as some theories of Shakespearian stagecraft suggest.

While texts dependent on playhouse copy provide important primary evidence for the study of staging, the converse is also true. Texts evidently not derived from the playhouse have no primary value as evidence for the study of staging. For example, in the case of a play printed from the author's foul papers or rough draft, some stage directions may represent the author's intentions not fully realized on stage. Greg describes the 1623 Folio text of *Timon of Athens* as "printed from foul papers that had never been reduced to anything like order.... There is no record of the play's having been acted, and it is most unlikely that it ever was.... Shakespeare's *Timon* is no finished play but an *ébauche.*"[13] With other plays the author apparently revised for the reader and sent to the printing house a text that he specified as non-theatrical. For example, in his prefatory epistle to the 1605 Quarto of *Sejanus,* Ben Jonson states: "I would informe you, that this Booke, in all numbers, is not the same with that which was acted on the publike Stage, wherein a second pen had good share; in place of which I have rather chosen, to put weaker (and no doubt lesse pleasing) of mine own, then to defraud so happy a *Genius* of his right, by my lothed usurpation." Here Jonson clearly distinguishes between two versions of the play: the authorial text he sent to the printer and the now lost theatrical text used for the play's unpopular and controversial performance.[14] Thus, while the 1623 *Timon* and the 1605 *Sejanus* are both authoritative texts, neither should be offered as primary evidence for the study of staging.

Bibliographical and textual scholars suggest that forty-two of the printed plays included as evidence for my study are printed from prompt copy or texts that may depend wholly or in part on prompt copy. Because dramatic texts of the period are of unequal value for the purposes of understanding stagecraft, at the head of each chapter I discuss in detail the staging requirements of the manuscripts and printed texts that may depend on playhouse

---

13 *The Shakespeare First Folio* (Oxford, 1955), p. 411.
14 Chambers, *Elizabethan Stage,* III, 366-368.

copy. I then summarize briefly the needs of plays that probably do not depend on playhouse copy.

The source of my checklist for plays first printed in the years 1600-1659 is W. W. Greg, *A Bibliography of the English Printed Drama to the Restoration.*[15] For the purposes of this study, I eliminated masques, pageants, and other texts that are not full-length plays in the sense that Shakespeare's works are plays. I also eliminated as evidence any plays probably first performed before late 1599 and plays for which evidence is lacking or inconclusive concerning a performance by professionals between late 1599 and September 1642.

During this period the royal and courtly influence on the drama increased and, as G. E. Bentley observes, a social cleavage developed in the London audiences.[16] The gentry and professional classes went to enclosed private playhouses such as Blackfriars and the Phoenix, while the lower classes went to open-air public playhouses such as the Globe and the Red Bull. Although these two kinds of playhouse differed in outward appearance, analysis of 276 plays probably first acted by professionals in this period shows that there were no significant differences in the staging requirements of the various companies and that the stage equipment needed was much simpler than has been thought. This study is therefore organized according to the increasing complexity of stage facilities required by the plays rather than according to the playhouse or the acting company. The plays fall into four groups, each with similar staging requirements.

First is a group of plays that can be acted in any hall or playhouse with minimal equipment: floor space in front of an unlocalized façade through which actors make their entrances and large properties can be *thrust out* or *brought on*. A second group of plays needs an additional acting place *above* the main stage, but this place is required in only one or two brief scenes in any given play. A third group needs an accessory space covered with doors or hangings where actors can hide, or where actors, or large properties, or both, can be brought into view. Here again, use is limited to one or two brief scenes in any given play. Finally, a group of plays needs a trap to the place *below* the stage. Of the 276 plays discussed, 121 were first acted by the King's Men, 155

[15] 4 vols. (London, 1939-1959).
[16] Bentley, *Shakespeare and His Theatre* (Lincoln, Nebr., 1964), p. 85.

by other companies. About half were first acted in 1599-1620, the other half in 1621-42.

It is important to emphasize that eighty-seven plays, or about one-third of the texts cited as evidence, make minimal demands and can be acted *without* an acting place above, doors or hangings, or a trap to the place below. This first group includes *Measure for Measure, King Lear, Twelfth Night,* and *As You Like It.* Stage direction references to *doors* in these plays—and in most plays discussed later—should be glossed in the early sense of "a passage into a building or room, a doorway." For example, a stage direction in *Twelfth Night* reads *Enter Viola and Malvolio, at severall doores* (II.ii), *"severall"* being used here in the sense of "distinct or apart" rather than "more than two." The only statement about locale in the text of this scene is Viola's comment that she has "since arriv'd but hither." As movable doors would serve no function here or elsewhere in the play, it seems likely that *severall doores* should be taken to mean two entrances such as those in the hall screen at the Middle Temple, where the play was acted on February 2, 1601/2. If we accept the premise that stage hangings can be parted to allow for entrances, then all the plays included in this first group can be acted on the stages shown in the extant pictorial evidence.

Other staging procedures discussed in this chapter also apply to plays discussed in later chapters. Stage directions often indicate that actors enter or exit in different directions, but the entrances themselves are localized only temporarily, if at all. The frequent use of the wording *at one door and . . . at the other* strongly suggests that playwrights of the period thought of the stage as having two entrances. Only five plays first acted by professionals in these years require more than two entrances; none of these texts appear to be printed from prompt copy. I interpret the direction *over the stage* to mean "enter at one door and exit the other." For example, Folio *King Lear* has *Alarum within. Enter with Drumme and Colours, Lear, Cordelia, and Souldiers, over the Stage, and Exeunt* (V.ii).

Large properties are required infrequently, rarely more than two in any given play. Most are commonplace household items simpler than many of the properties listed in Henslowe's *Diary* or in the Revels Accounts.[17] Many are described as *brought on* by

---

[17] See R. A. Foakes and R. T. Rickert, eds., *Henslowe's Diary* (Cambridge, 1961), *passim*; Albert Feuillerat, "Documents Relating to the Office of the Revels in the

servants or *set out*, presumably by stage keepers. These properties include Banquets, Tables and Chairs, Stools, a Bar of Justice, a Bed, a Hearse or Coffin, a Tomb, and miscellaneous other properties such as *Stocks brought out* in *King Lear* (II.ii. 146).

In addition to entrances and large properties, the forty-five plays considered in the next chapter need an acting place above the main playing area. Occasionally this space may be described fictionally as a *window* or the *walls*, but more often it is referred to theatrically as *above* or *aloft*. It usually serves during a brief scene as an observation post from which one or two actors comment on, or converse with, actors down on the main stage. This area should therefore be considered as an auxiliary to the main stage rather than a distinct and separate "upper stage." All nine façades in the pictorial and architectural evidence have an elevated area suitable for this kind of limited action.

In scenes in which actors move backstage from the area above to the main playing area—or vice versa—lines are spoken by those on stage to cover the time elapsing. In *Othello*, Roderigo and Iago call to Brabantio, who appears *Above* at I.i.81 and exits at l.144. Iago then speaks to Roderigo for sixteen lines and exits, at which point *Enter Brabantio, with Servants and Torches*. In *Julius Caesar*, Cassius orders Pindarus to "get higher on that hill" (V.ii.20) so that he may better see what happens to Titinius; *Pindarus Above* reports that Titinius is "enclosed round about" (l.28).

In some plays actors apparently remain in full view of the audience as they ascend to, or descend from, the acting area above the stage. Of the texts that may depend on prompt copy, only Shakespeare's *Cymbeline* calls for an elaborate descent: *Jupiter descends in Thunder and Lightning, sitting uppon an Eagle: hee throwes a Thunder-bolt. The Ghostes fall on their knees* (V.iv.92). After his speech of twenty-one lines Jupiter *Ascends*. Although there is some evidence for elaborate apparatus to "fly" actors and large

---

Time of Queen Elizabeth," in W. Bang, ed., *Materialen zur kunde des alteren Englischen Dramas*, XXI (Louvain, 1908), *passim*; Albert Feuillerat, "Documents Relating to the Revels at Court in the Time of King Edward VI and Queen Mary" (The Losely MSS.), in W. Bang, ed., *Materialen zur kunde des alteren Englischen Dramas*, XLIV (Louvain, 1914), *passim*.

properties in the Italian theatre of the period, evidence for its use in the English theatre is meagre.

C. Walter Hodges reproduces a drawing for flying machinery that "may have been copied from the work of the famous Giacomo Torelli at a theatre in Venice between 1640 and 1645."[18] Concerning the use of such equipment on the English stage, John Cranford Adams cites Ben Jonson's Prologue for *Every Man in His Humour* (Folio, 1616): "Where neither Chorus wafts you ore the seas/ Nor creaking throne comes downe the boys to please," and stage directions in Greene's *Alphonsus of Aragon*, which Chambers dates c. 1587 without conjecture about company or playhouse: *After you have sounded thrise, let Venus be let downe, from the top of the Stage, and when she is downe say . . . Exit Venus. Or if you can conveniently, let a chaire come downe, from the top of the stage, and draw her up.*[19]

Stage directions for only five plays first performed between 1599 and 1642 require actors, or large properties, or both, to ascend to or descend from the acting area above; none of these texts makes explicit references to stage machinery, however. Thus, while it cannot be proven that such machinery did not exist, it can be stated with some certainty that such machinery was not *required* in the vast majority of plays. This strongly suggests that such machinery was not available in the majority of playhouses. It therefore seems that a more likely means of staging ascents and descents would be a movable staircase set in place for the scenes in which it is required. *The Knight of Malta*—a King's Men play c. 1616— contains a notation apparently printed from prompt copy: *The Scaffold set out and the staires* (II.v). These are also mentioned in Henslowe's inventory of properties for the Lord Admiral's Men dated March 10, 1598, at which time the company was playing at the Rose: "i payer of stayers for Fayeton." Henslowe's *Diary* shows that Dekker was given four pounds for "a booke... called fayeton" on January 15, 1597/8.[20] This text is lost, but if the dramatization followed the familiar myth, stairs may have been put in place for

---

[18] Hodges, p. 117.
[19] As cited by Adams, *The Globe Playhouse*, 2nd ed. (New York, 1961), p. 335.
[20] *Henslowe's Diary*, pp. 86, 319.

Phaeton's ascent to the area above and his subsequent descent.[21]

One hundred and two plays, or about one-third of those included as evidence, need an accessory stage space covered with doors or hangings, where actors can hide, or where actors, or large properties, or both can be *discovered*. Here *discover* has the sense of "to disclose, or expose to view anything covered up or previously unseen." Of these 102 plays, forty-six also need an acting area above. In a few plays, stage directions specify that a movable door is closed or locked, or that it is opened to make discovery. Many more plays call for concealment by curtains, hangings, or an arras; these are drawn or parted. Since doors and hangings so often serve the same functions, that is, concealment and disclosure, they were probably used interchangeably, depending on what may have been available at a given hall or playhouse. Again we note that hangings may have been put in place for special scenes only.

The accessory space is used frequently as a hiding place for one actor. The dialogue of *The Winter's Tale* (V.iii) refers to "curtains" and *Hermione (like a statue)* is probably brought into view at Pauline's line. "Behold and say tis well" (1.20). Falstaff *stands behind the aras* in Quarto *The Merry Wives of Windsor* (III.iii.99).

The space may be localized for a brief scene, but action flows to and from the main playing area and usually the scene ends with the familiar *exeunt*. For example, the Folio text of *Troilus and Cressida* has *Enter Achilles and Patroclus in their tent* (III.iii.37). This is followed by Ulysses' comment "Achilles stands i' th entrance of his Tent," which makes it clear that the primary action of the scene takes place on the main stage and not within the "tent." This space is localized in other plays as a *closet*, a *shop*, or a *study*, but since entire scenes are not played within the confines of this space, it should not be thought of as an "inner stage." This is a misleading term of recent coinage that is not used in any pre-Restoration play.

---

[21] In Shakespeare's *Richard II* (first printed 1597), the King *on the walls* is summoned to "the base court" to meet with Bolingbroke. Richard's speech beginning "Down, down I come, like glist'ring Phaeton" (III.iii.186) may be given as he descends on a stairway in view of the audience. In all the early texts of the play Richard remains on stage until *exeunt* at the end of the scene. Capell (1768) and later editors emend with *Exeunt from above* (1.191) and *Enter King Richard and his Attendants below* (1.195).

Finally, forty-two plays require a trap to a place below, which necessitates a platform stage. Many of these plays also require an acting area above, or hangings, or both. For example, *Hamlet* has *Ghost cries under the Stage* (I.v.149) and Polonius hides behind the arras where he is killed (III.iv). This scene ends with *Exit Hamlet tugging in Polonius*. After the burial of Ophelia, Laertes *Leaps in the grave* (V.i.273). In *Macbeth* the use of a trap is strongly implied by the stage direction *Witches vanish*, followed by Banquo's line "The earth hath bubbles, as the Water ha's" (I.iii.78). A trap would also be useful for Banquo's Ghost who appears and vanishes in the Banquet scene (III.iv) and for the three Apparitions who speak and then *descend* (IV.i). Similar vanishing acts are found in *The Two Noble Kinsmen*, where the *Hynde vanishes under the Altar* (V.i.162), and in *Cymbeline*, where Ghosts *vanish* (V.iv.122). In *The Tempest* Ariel *vanishes in Thunder* (III.iii.82), and later the figures of the masque *heavily vanish* (IV.i.138). The trap is sometimes described fictionally as a *well*, a *gulf*, a *ditch*, or a *vault*.

In summary, the basic requirement for the performance of Shakespeare's plays is an unlocalized façade through which actors can enter and large properties can be *brought on* or *thrust out*. Some plays need a supplementary acting area above for a brief scene or two; others need an accessory space covered with doors or hangings for a brief scene or two; still others need a trap to the place below the stage. It should be remembered, however, that most plays did not require all of these facilities and that actors may have improvised according to the stage facilities available to them.

I hope that my study may extend the structure of valid inference concerning the pre-Restoration stage. More important, I hope it will help to limit the field of admissible conjecture. Perhaps readers of Shakespeare's plays can be freed once and for all from the misconception that his plays were acted in a setting that in any way represented "a street," or "a room at the castle," or "another part of the forest." Shakespeare's plays were acted with a minimum of equipment on an unlocalized open stage. I hope that modern producers of Shakespeare's plays will be encouraged to follow this simple, flexible mode of production. If so, we may gain a better understanding of the original theatrical values in this astonishing body of dramatic literature.

Three Times *Ho*
and a Brace of Widows:
Some Plays for the
Private Theatre

CLIFFORD LEECH

I have the vividest recollection of the first Waterloo conference on the Elizabethan theatre two years ago, but last year I listened to a voice calling "Westward Ho" and therefore could not come. Perhaps it was because of a sense of having missed things then that on this occasion I have decided to talk to you mainly on the group of plays that began with the *Westward Ho* of Dekker and Webster of 1604. For whatever reason, however, it seems useful to look at three plays that show the private theatre of the seventeenth century's first decade, each of the later ones recalling what had been done before, all of them manifesting to some extent a common outlook, expecting their audience to be familiar with what was going on at the other private theatre, and with more than an occasional nod at the popular triumphs of the public stage. Not that I want to suggest a firm dichotomy between public and private: that, I believe, was a phenomenon of the last thirty years before the Civil War, although even then it is evident from Volume VI of G. E. Bentley's *The Jacobean and Caroline Stage* (Oxford, 1968) that there was free interplay between public and private as far as actors were concerned.[1] In the century's first decade, *The Malcontent* could be taken over by the King's Men;

[1] See, for example, 170, 219.

Troilus and Cressida was probably written for an Inns of Court—
and therefore private—performance; *Timon of Athens*, it has recently been argued by Professor Muriel Bradbrook, was essentially a private-theatre play, written for the King's Men's new
stage at the Blackfriars.[2] It has to be remembered that London,
in relation to anything we know today, was still a comparatively
small town, although one of the largest in Europe. Giovanni
Butero, writing about 1590, classes it with Naples, Lisbon, Prague,
and Ghent as possessing about 160,000 inhabitants, more or less.[3]
It was, in fact, a place where each literate man was likely to have
some familiarity with everything that was going on. Yet, when we
consider the three plays, *Westward Ho, Eastward Ho*, and
Northward Ho, we are conscious of coming into touch with an
in-group whose members rivalled each other, could even show
respect for each other as well as an occasional mockery, could
make in-jokes which its audience could be expected to take up.
The private-theatre audience manifestly frequented also the
public theatre at this time, but the reverse cannot have been
wholly true. At Paul's and the Blackfriars you could have a sense
of being at the club: the *profanum vulgus* was without, and
could be safely mocked.

The compliment of being asked to address this conference
provides the opportunity to give further thought to what
I have rather cavalierly said in earlier years. In 1966 I was asked
to speak at the Conference on Research Opportunities in
Renaissance Drama, held at the MLA convention, and
chose as my theme the way that Elizabethan and Jacobean
dramatists were often influenced by what had been immediately successful in the theatre of their time—not simply in
order to follow popular taste, but because what had just
previously been done opened up a new way of dramatic
composition. My main point in relation to what I shall call
the *Ho* plays was that Dekker and Webster in *Westward
Ho* modified the old "journeying" play, which went back as
far as the dramatic romances that Sidney made fun of in his

---

[2] *Shakespeare the Craftsman* (London, 1969), ch. VIII.

[3] *Encyclopaedia Britannica*, ninth edition (Edinburgh, reprinted 1898), XIV, 820.
Alfred Harbage, *Shakespeare's Audience* (New York, 1941; reprinted 1961),
argues for 160,000 "for the population of the entire metropolitan area of London
served by the theatres in 1605" (p. 41). T. F. Reddaway, "London and the Court,"
Shakespeare Survey 17 (Cambridge, 1964), suggests a figure between 200,000 and
250,000 for 1603 (p. 3).

Clifford Leech

Apology, by making the journey the smallest conceivable one, from London to Brentford, and insisting on the unchanging mores of the main characters, the essential unchangeability of their situation; the old journeying play, like *The Two Gentlemen of Verona*, could lead to a genuine change of heart. Chapman, Jonson and Marston took over the pattern in *Eastward Ho*, there mocking fairly overtly the old idea of transformation, and Dekker and Webster made a further, though altogether less successful, attempt to repeat their former success in *Northward Ho*.[4] And all the time the two groups of dramatists wrote with an eye on each other: *Eastward Ho's* prologue refers to *Westward Ho*, and I think the play also makes fun of a major success of Dekker in the public theatre; *Northward Ho* includes an obvious caricature of Chapman, one of *Eastward Ho's* writers.

It is important to remember how close in date these plays are. *Westward Ho* came in 1604 at Paul's, *Eastward Ho* in 1605 at the Blackfriars, *Northward Ho* also in 1605 at Paul's. As each of the two later plays was seen, the memory of the others must have been firmly in the audience's minds.

What I especially want to do on this occasion is to pursue further the links between the three plays, to see also what evidence they give us for staging at the private theatres, and to underline their community of outlook. Of course, *Eastward Ho* is by far the best of the three, although I believe it has, until recently, been the one least understood. When I have said what I have to say on this group, I want to add a few remarks on Chapman's *The Widow's Tears*—a play that may not be far in date from the *Ho* plays, that was written by one of the authors of *Eastward Ho*, and that shows something in common with *Eastward Ho's* staging.

Let us begin, then, with *Westward Ho*, the first of the *Ho* trio. Dekker and Webster were perhaps much about the same age,[5] but Webster seems to have come slowly to dramatic writing, while in 1604 Dekker was already established. The only earlier work by Webster that we can be reasonably sure of is his collaboration with Dekker on *The Famous*

[4] "The Dramatists' Independence," *RORD*, X (1967), 17-23.
[5] No certain birthdate is known for either: currently accepted approximations are c. 1572 for Dekker, and c. 1575 for Webster. See Alfred Harbage, *Annals of English Drama, 975-1700*, rev. S. Schoenbaum (London, 1964), pp. 221, 229.

History of Sir Thomas Wyatt in about 1602, and his additions
to *The Malcontent* when it was taken over by the King's
Men in 1604. But Dekker had made a powerful mark in both
public and private theatres: *Old Fortunatus, The Shoemaker's
Holiday, Patient Grissel, Sir Thomas Wyatt,* and Part I of
The Honest Whore were played publicly, with dates ranging
from 1599 to 1604; *Satiromastix,* perhaps written in 1601 in
collaboration with Marston, was done at both Paul's and the
Globe. Moreover, in *The Shoemaker's Holiday* Dekker had
made himself very much of a dramatist for the London
citizens: when Simon Eyre entertains the King, he, as Lord
Mayor, is, if not an equal, yet still a self-respecting host. As
much as Heywood in *The Four Prentices of London,* first
acted probably sometime between 1592 and 1600, he proclaims
the glory of the city. But now in *Westward Ho* he will make
fun of it, at least to some extent, being willing to enter the
world of the private theatre again and to laugh at the world
outside.

And yet not quite. There are two separate actions in
Westward Ho, one acting as framework for the other, and
the framing-action shows city virtue triumphant. It tells of
an Italian merchant, Justiniano, who has lost a good deal
of his money and is jealous of the attentions that his wife is
receiving from an old earl. His remedy is to tell his wife he has
lost everything and will go abroad; she may do as she
pleases. She accepts the rich clothes the earl offers and goes
to his house. But there her virtue triumphs and she writes
to her husband to tell him so. There follows a grotesque se-
duction scene, where the earl finds that all his fine talk is
wasted because he has been addressing Justiniano himself
dressed in the clothes the earl has intended that Justiniano's
wife should wear. This causes one of those moments of conversion that Middleton made fun of so frequently in his city
comedies. Here there is no question of fun, and all the intense
moments are presented in blank verse. Aristocracy is quite
seriously humbled.

Meanwhile, Justiniano has been busy in another disguise.
He assumes the role of Parenthesis, a writing-teacher, and
acts as apparent bawd to three city wives. They meet three
gallants in a tavern, and arrange for a rendezvous with them
at Brentford, which means of course that they go westward

17

from London. The husbands are themselves unfaithful with a whore, Luce, and one of the best scenes in the play is that in which they appear successively at her lodging. But at Brentford the wives decide to stay virtuous; one of them pretends to be sick, so the women spend the night together in one room, the gallants in another. Justiniano brings the husbands along; they are convinced of their wives' virtue, and shamed when Luce's bawd reveals their own unfaithfulness. This main part of the play is an ambiguous tribute to city virtue, but Dekker and Webster manage to combine making fun of the citizen class without suggesting any infidelity on the part of the wives. At the end of the first scene, Justiniano avers that city dames are "the fittest, and most proper persons for a Comedy," but he continues:

> Court, Citty, and Countrey, are meerely as maskes one to the other, envied of some, laught at of others, and so to my comicall businesse. (I.i.227-9)[6]

Moreover, if citizens are not treated too easily, neither are the Inns of Court men. The termers, who must have been present at Paul's, do not escape scot-free in the scene between Luce and her bawd, Mistress Birdlime:

> *Luce* ... what a filthy knocking was at doore last night; some puny Inn-a-court-men, Ile hold my contribution.
> *Bird.* Yes in troth were they, civill gentlemen without beards, but to say the truth, I did take exceptions at their knocking: took them a side and said to them: Gentlemen this is not well, that you should come in this habit, Cloakes and Rapiers, Boots and Spurs, I protest to you, those that be your Ancientes in the house would have come to my house in their Caps and Gownes, civilly, and modestly. I promise you they might have bin taken for Cittizens, but that they talke more liker fooles. (IV.i.9-18)

Of course, the termers would be happier because the benchers were thus put slightly below the citizen rank.

Apart from the earnest scenes between the earl and Justiniano's wife, the play is wholly in prose. One of the things that we should, I think, note in the first decade of the

---

[6] Quotations from *Westward Ho* and *Northward Ho* are from *The Dramatic Works of Thomas Dekker*, ed. Fredson Bowers, 4 vols. (Cambridge, 1953-61).

seventeenth century is that the private theatres came near to establishing prose as the predominant comic medium.

But *Westward Ho*, like its successors, was also a play about plays. I suspect that, when Justiniano speaks to one of the city wives, he is made deliberately to echo Iago's address to Brabantio in the first scene of *Othello*. Iago says:

> Even now, now, very now, an old blacke Ram
> Is tupping your white Ewe.[7] (I.96)

Justiniano has this:

> why, even now, now, at holding up of this finger, and before the turning downe of this, some are murdring, some lying with their maides, some picking of pockets, some cutting purses, some cheating, some weying out bribes. In this Citty some wives are Cuckolding some Husbands. (II.i.186-90)

Interestingly enough, this passage seems to be echoed by Tourneur — or whoever else wrote *The Revenger's Tragedy*, a play surely firm enough in our repertory since the Royal Shakespeare Theatre has revived it so splendidly — where, in perhaps the following year, Vindice was given these words:

> Now 'tis full sea abed over the world;
> There's juggling of all sides. Some that were maids
> E'en at sunset are now perhaps i' th' toll-book.
> This woman in immodest thin apparel
> Lets in her friend by water; here a dame,
> Cunning, nails leather hinges to a door,
> To avoid proclamation; now cuckolds are
> A-coining, apace, apace, apace, apace . . .[8] (II.ii.136-43)

But *Westward Ho* could also look back to *The Spanish Tragedy*, referring to "old *Ieronimo*; goe by, go by" (II.ii.185), and a mention in the same scene of the "very dangerous" way over Gadshill suggests that *I Henry IV* was to be remembered by the audience. In the last act the quite recent *Hamlet* was also referred to: "let these husbands play mad *Hamlet*, and crie revenge" (V.iv.50-51).

---

[7] This is the Folio reading. The Quartos (see the new Arden edition) read: "Even now, very now."
[8] *The Revenger's Tragedy*, ed. R. A. Foakes, Revels Plays (London, 1966).

Clifford Leech

Manifestly, the play was a considerable success. If it had not been, Blackfriars would not have thought of a *riposte*. Chapman, Jonson and Marston produced *Eastward Ho* in the following year, using for their title the other famous watermens' cry on the Thames. It is no part of my concern here to discuss the trouble that befell the three dramatists because of their comments on the Scots, except to note that this underlies the essentially satiric character of the play. Nor, here as with the other *Ho* plays, shall I comment on the speculative apportionment of the text among the collaborators. That the Blackfriars group were not writing in animosity towards *Westward Ho* is apparent enough from the prologue. There seems no reason not to take its opening lines at their face value:

> Not out of envy, for there's no effect
> Where there's no cause; nor out of imitation,
> For we have evermore been imitated;
> Nor out of our contention to do better
> Than that which is oppos'd to ours in title,
> For that was good; and better cannot be ... (Prologue, 1-6)[9]

Yet the old view of *Eastward Ho* was that it was staunchly moral in opposition to *Westward Ho*. Here is Thomas Marc Parrott, Chapman's distinguished editor, on the subject:

Eastward Ho, in its main outlines at least, seems to me a conscious protest of such moralists against the new comedy of Middleton and Dekker. It adopts their realistic treatment, excludes all trace of romance or sentiment, and presents a picture of city life completely convincing in its verisimilitude. But in strong distinction from the work of Middleton and Dekker this picture is one of honesty, industry, and sobriety victorious over roguery, idleness, and dissipation. Touchstone, the real hero of the play, a thorough-going citizen with all the citizen's limitations, is another guess figure than Quomodo or Justinian. There is no dallying with vice in his household, and if, against his will, one night is given up to wasteful prodigality, it is atoned for in the morning by the expulsion of the typical prodigal. In other words instead of the laxness and confusion of morals which we have noted in

[9] Quotations from *Eastward Ho* and *The Widow's Tears* are from *The Plays of George Chapman*, ed. Thomas Marc Parrott, 4 vols. (London, 1910-14; reprinted New York, 1961).

20

Westward Ho, we have here a sharp differentiation between vice and virtue, — the latter, to be sure, presented in a somewhat bourgeois form — an open conflict, and the final triumph of the good. (*Comedies*,II,840)

We may discern a slight reservation when Parrott says "in its main outlines at least" and "presented in a somewhat bourgeois form"; even so, he is arguing strenuously for the play's face value. Nor do C. H. Herford and Percy Simpson take a very different view. Of Touchstone they say that he

> is a citizen in the strictest sense. He is not a whit raised above his order; but he has all the thrifty virtues of the honest tradesman, and they are honoured and vindicated in him, instead of being derided.[10]

They rightly see that the story has relations to the early Prodigal Son plays, but regard Golding as a particularly attractive presentation of the elder brother figure:

> by judiciously blending the sterner and the milder traditions of the subject they have both given Goulding [*sic*] a role of much dramatic strength, and made him personally more attractive, in spite of much unction, than it has usually been given to the descendants of the "elder brother" to be.

Still they do thus admit "much unction," and add:

> But the character is somewhat outside the Elizabethan beat, and is nowhere in the play, we think, managed with perfect security and ease. A nice scrutiny may perhaps even detect some hesitation or inconsistency in the language put into his mouth.[11]

Moreover, they remark that Quicksilver's conversion is "not made dramatically plausible." If Herford and Simpson slightly hesitated, it has been for recent critics to come out plainly with the view that *Eastward Ho* is throughout a splendid and good-humoured satire on city virtues, that Quicksilver is of course foolish but is also great dramatic fun, that nothing is to be taken seriously here. Anthony Caputi, in his book *John Marston, Satirist*

---

[10] *Ben Jonson*, ed. C. H. Herford, Percy and Evelyn Simpson (Oxford, 1925), II, 33.
[11] e.g., I.ii.58, 77, 85, II.ii.144.

Clifford Leech

(Ithaca, N.Y., 1961), has in particular written shrewdly on the play. I should like to quote a few sentences from his discussion:

> Golding and Mildred muddle on, aglow with virtue and hard work....
> The crowning merit of *Eastward Ho* is that all of its parts are contrived so that each contributes maximally to the comic and satiric effect of the whole. This merit is, perhaps, most clearly seen in the major controls placed on the action. What might pass for relatively serious villainy in many another comedy, for example, is here rendered nonserious by the treatment of the villains.... Throughout *Eastward Ho*, accordingly, the satire is double-edged, cutting finely but surely into the complacency of Touchstone and his group just as it cuts into the humorous extravagance of Sir Petronel and his associates.... Golding and Mildred are so excessively thrifty and modest in all things that ambition in them seems deprived of desire. The explicit norms of behaviour established by Touchstone, Golding, and Mildred, consequently, are as comic as the deviations from them. The over-all effect of this instability is that the world of *Eastward Ho* shimmers with a comic unity exhilarating to behold. (pp. 224-26.)

More recently still, Muriel Bradbrook has included *Eastward Ho* in the type of "that new bitter comedy where morality was mocked" and has labelled it "a parody of the usual prodigal play" (op. cit. pp. 154, 180). The word "bitter" seems out of place here, and the play is surely much more than a parody, but we cannot deny a strong element of parody in it.

What we may notice first here is that in *Eastward Ho* there is nothing corresponding to the scenes between the earl and Justiniano's wife in *Westward Ho*. There is, of course, Quicksilver's ballad of repentance, but that is surely to be taken no more seriously than the reprieve of Macheath in *The Beggar's Opera*. We should note that Quicksilver's ballad is not to be interrupted. When Touchstone feels moved by the ballad, he is prevented from intervening before it is ended; Wolf an officer of the Counter, prevents him in an aside to Golding: "Stay him, Master Deputy; now is the time; we shall lose the song else" (V.v. 86-7). And, soon after, the usurer Security sings his own ridiculous song of repentance (V.v.145-54). This play, unlike its predecessor, is all of a piece; throughout, it asserts the profitability of city virtue, while making fun of it and the perils incident to unthrift, while making the unthrifty quite delightful. It takes over the journey-idea, but in a paradoxical fashion. Sir Petronel Flash

22

and his companions travel eastwards in order to reach Virginia, and get only as far as Cuckold's Haven; Gertrude travels to a non-existent castle; Golding makes the short step from his master's shop to the hall of his city company. For Webster's and Dekker's one short journey to Brentford we have these three much shorter ones. The play takes over the city characters of its predecessor, too, and overtly holds up Touchstone, Golding and Mildred as admirable. But the names of Touchstone and Golding and their occupation should make us a little suspicious. Shakespeare had used the name Touchstone a few years before, but his Touchstone was a tester of wit: the Touchstone here is a tester, immediately of gold, incidentally of moral fibre. And gold after all had come under strong suspicion lately, and was to be the great corrupter in *Volpone, The Alchemist* and *Timon of Athens*. The Blackfriars audience in 1605 was not likely to see the goldsmith's as the least dubious of occupations.

Further, I should draw attention to the fact that this is quite a bawdy play. In rereading it, I have noted numerous examples of bawdiness, though there is not time now to give a complete, and doubtless delectable, list. Even so, in the very first scene Touchstone uses bawdiness without knowing it (a sure way of "placing" the character). It is the old joke of the horn, given here a point because what Touchstone himself has in mind is only the cornucopia:

> And when I was wived, having something to stick to, I had the horn of
> suretyship ever before my eyes. You all know the device of the horn,
> where the young fellow slips in at the butt-end, and comes squeezed
> out at the buccal: and I grew up, and I praise Providence, I bear my
> brows now as high as the best of my neighbours... (I.i.50-6).

In a similar way we have puns on "member" and "country lady" and "prick," in Gertrude's begging Sir Petronel to take her to his castle, using the words, "I beseech thee down with me, for God's sake" (I.ii.128), in Quicksilver's comment on Security's abbreviating his wife's name to Winnie ("That's all he can do, poor man, he may well cut off her name at Winnie" [II.ii.203-4]), and in many others of Quicksilver's speeches. The audience must have been kept busy laughing. Even today there are some scholars specializing in Elizabethan–Jacobean drama who are strangely unaware of double entendres. One of my favourite remarks concerning my much-valued editors in the Revels series is that some fail to see bawdiness anywhere, and some see it everywhere. I don't think I belong with the latter, but this play is surely thick with it.

Let us, however, get back to Touchstone. Madame M. T. Jones-Davies in her *Un Peintre de la Vie Londonienne: Thomas Dekker* (Paris, 1958) has rightly recognized a connection between him and Simon Eyre in *The Shoemaker's Holiday,* which, we have noted, had been acted some years before and had had a great success in the public theatre. Eyre, like Touchstone, was a city craftsman and rose to even higher office than Touchstone's Golding did. He was masterful, as Touchstone is. He was garrulous, as Touchstone is: he had his favourite phrase, "Prince am I none, yet am I princely borne" (which Dekker took over from Deloney), as Touchstone has his "Work upon that now!" For Madame Jones-Davies we have here a simple echo; taking her cue from Herford and Simpson (II.33), she declares:

> Touchstone fait honneur à la condition bourgeoise, mais pour autant ne manque ni d'humour ni de pittoresque. Il se rattache à la race de Sim Eyre, c'est-à-dire de l'artisan sympathique que Dekker, le premier, a révélé sur la scène. (II.286)

And, for all the good humour of the prologue to *Eastward Ho,* I think that Herford and Simpson and Madame Jones-Davies have missed the point. Jonson previously had brought Marston on to the stage in *Poetaster* in the person of Crispinus; Jonson, Chapman and Marston, following on a play written by the well-known Dekker, the much less well-known Webster (at this date), could parody the most famous figure that Dekker had created. It is true that some of us today may think that Eyre ought to have been ambivalently regarded, and that it is a shortcoming of *The Shoemaker's Holiday* that he does not seem to be so regarded there. My colleague, William Blissett, to whom I owe so much from our discussions of Elizabethan–Jacobean drama, has recently remarked to me that Touchstone is not the "monster" that Eyre is; and to modify the "monster" was surely a right thing for the dramatists of *Eastward Ho* to do; Touchstone fits admirably into the good-humoured pattern of this play. The surest way to make the Blackfriars audience aware that the dramatists were concerned with burlesque was to give to his favourite daughter and his favourite apprentice the language of the Puritans. They go fairly far here, and bring to mind Jonson's prologue to the performance of *Bartholomew Fair* at court, when he frankly states that James, like the players, has suffered from "your land's Faction." Listen to Mildred:

> I had rather make up the garment of my affections in some of the same piece, than, like a fool, wear gowns of two colours, and mix sackcloth with satin. (II.i.56-8)

But one of the most frequent expressions in the play, rivalling Touchstone's "Work upon that now!" is the biblical "hunger and thirst after" (Matthew, V, 6). At the end of Act II, Scene iii, Gertrude says to Sir Petronel: "Come, sweet knight, come; I do hunger and thirst to be abed with thee," (II.iii.172-3). So at the end of Act III, Scene i, Security, the usurer, says: "I do hunger and thirst to do you good, sir!"; in Act III, Scene ii, Sir Petronel, looking to enjoy another woman, says: "I thirst and hunger / To taste the dear feast of her company," and goes on to refer to "the hunger and the thirst" that Security had vowed to devote to the accomplishment of Sir Petronel's wishes; when the would-be voyagers are exuberantly together before they set out, two of them, wanting to share the toast to Sir Petronel's mistress, cry: "We do hunger and thirst for it." All this repetition is as near blasphemy as might delight Blackfriars.

It is Quicksilver who speaks the epilogue, as Volpone and Face were to speak the epilogues for their plays. This is customarily a sign of a dramatist's favour, and a sign, too, that he expects the character to be prominently in the audience's hearts. But if we needed a further comment on Quicksilver's "conversion," we could find it in his special triumph recorded by Wolf, the officer of the Counter; he tells us that Quicksilver has converted "one Fangs, a sergeant," has taught him to pare his nails and say his prayers, and, in culmination, "'tis hoped he will sell his place shortly, and become an intelligencer" (V.ii.59-63). To become an intelligencer is the kind of promotion that Shakespeare's Pompey received when, from a bawd, he became an executioner's assistant.

In one other respect this play keeps to the *Westward Ho* pattern: it is a play about plays. There was nothing new in this, of course. We can especially remember Ancient Pistol. But *Eastward Ho* makes the "in-group" joke many times. Quicksilver quotes *Tamburlaine*, the lost play *Hiren*, Chapman's own *The Blind Beggar of Alexandria*, *The Spanish*

Tragedy. Above all, *Hamlet* is referred to. Golding urges that the leftovers from Gertrude's feast will do for the marriage-banquet for him and Mildred:

> Let me beseech you, no, sir; the superfluity and cold meat left at their nuptials will with bounty furnish ours. (II.ii.157-9)

And in Act III, Scene ii, a footman named Hamlet refers to "My lady's coach," thus recalling Ophelia's last words, which are echoed again in Gertrude's demands for her coach some twenty lines later:

> *Ger.*   Thank you, good people! My coach, for the love of heaven, my coach! In good truth I shall swoun else.
> *Ham.*   Coach, coach, my lady's coach!   *Exit*
> *Ger.*   As I am a lady, I think I am with child already, I long for a coach so. (III.ii.27-31)

Later we are again told, as Quicksilver addresses Gertrude, "that the cold meat left at your wedding might serve to furnish their nuptial table" (III.ii.60-1), and Gertrude sings an Ophelia song:

> *His head as white as milk, all flaxen was his hair;*
> *But now he is dead, and laid in his bed,*
> *And never will come again.* (III.ii.77-9)

Appropriately enough, Touchstone, Golding and Mildred enter immediately, "*with rosemary*." Even *Richard III* is not left out, for Security cries "A boat, a boat, a boat," echoing Richard's cry for a horse. *Hamlet* again comes in when Slitgut, observing from above, sees a woman in the Thames below:

> Ay me, see another remnant of this unfortunate shipwrack, or some other! A woman, i'faith, a woman! Though it be almost at St. Katherine's, I discern it to be a woman, for all her body is above the water, and her clothes swim about her most handsomely. O, they bear her up most bravely! Has not a woman reason to love the taking up of her clothes the better while she lives, for this? (IV.i.57-63)

We have to remember Ophelia here, as we do later in a rather similar situation in *The Two Noble Kinsmen*. The bawdiness in the last words makes the echo all the more pungent, and we may note Parrott's gloss that St. Katherine's hospital "was used at this time as a reformatory for fallen women" (II.857). Eric Partridge, moreover, tells us that Kate was a common name for a whore,[12] and a Katherine was a kind of pear,[13] which has been a bawdy fruit ever since Mercutio referred to one variety of it. The Blackfriars was getting its own back, not merely on *Westward Ho*, but on the great successes of the public theatre.

Northward Ho is, comparatively, a disappointment. First, it departed perforce from the Thames' watermen's cries (thus indicating something of an effort to maintain the fun). Like *Westward Ho*, it took its city wives on a journey— this time to Ware, northwards, where again virtue was technically preserved, despite the legendary great bed which, of course, does not escape mention. It has neither the sentimental complexity of *Westward Ho* nor the astringent burlesque of *Eastward Ho*. Not surprisingly, it was the last of the group to be written: no one cared to write a *Southward Ho* afterwards. But, if Chapman, Jonson and Marston could make fun of Simon Eyre, Webster and Dekker could make fun of Chapman, and in Bellamont they did, referring to the play *Caesar and Pompey*, which he was doubtless talking about when they wrote but did not finish till much later.[14] He is presented, absurdly enough, as also planning a tragedy on Astyanax. He is made to talk much of French affairs, and in speeches by and to him "the Duke of *Biron*" and "Duke *Pepper-noone*" are mentioned, which suggests that Chapman was also talking about *Charles Duke of Byron*, which was to be acted in three years' time. There is an obvious echo of *Eastward Ho* when Greenshield "*disguised*" brings his wife to the gallants in Act V, Scene i. And again there are several references to plays, although not so specifically as in *Westward Ho* and *Eastward Ho*. Bellamont, the Chapman-figure, refers to "lattin Comedies" and to his being able to "make an excellent description of it [i.e., a scene he has observed] in a Comedy" (I.i.41, 54-5); and in Act I, Scene iii,

[12] *Shakespeare's Bawdy* (London, 1948; reprinted London, 1968), p. 129.
[13] Cf. *Bartholomew Fair*, ed. E. A. Horsman, Revels Plays (London, 1960), I.v.116.
[14] Cf. John Russell Brown, "Chapman's 'Caesar and Pompey': An Unperformed Play?" *MLR*, XLIX (1954), 466-69.

he offers to bring Master Mayberry's wife upon the stage and to have her husband play "a jealous mans part." When, in Act IV, Scene i, he thinks Doll will be coming to him, he thinks in terms of the stage:

> The letter saies here, that she's exceeding sick, and intreates me to visit her: Captaine, lie you in ambush behind the hangings [perhaps an echo of *Hamlet* again], and perhaps you shall heare the peece of a Commedy...(IV.i.115-17)

The term "comedy" is repeated later in this scene (ll.208-11), where the genre is compared to "a Canterbury tale," and in Act V, Scene i, where it is used in relation to the present play's denouement. Finally, there is a reference to "a company of country plaiers, that are come to towne here" (V.i.82-3). So what we may call the *Ho* mode was kept up, but the end had clearly been reached.

Chapman's *The Widow's Tears* may have followed in the same year. Samuel Schoenbaum's revision of Alfred Harbage's *Annals of English Drama 975-1700* gives 1605 as the most likely date, with a possible spread from 1603 to 1609. It was first published in 1612 "as often presented in the blacke and white Friers." It seems to belong with the *Ho* plays in its sardonic temper, although it is totally different from them in locale and in its use of an old story, that of the widow of Ephesus. It is, moreover, a play that uses the resources of the stage rather more freely than the plays we have been looking at. *Westward Ho* requires an "*above*" (IV.i.57.1), when Tenterhooke and Luce appear there, and in *Eastward Ho* Winifred appears "*above*" when she first addresses her husband in Act II, Scene ii. So, superbly, does Slitgut observe the lost travellers on the Thames in Act IV, Scene i: it is in the original stage direction, as in the previous examples cited, that he is said to be "*above*." In *Northward Ho* there is no such stage direction, and we have no reason to think that anyone appeared above the general stage level. But what we do have to believe is that in at least two of these plays there could be a substantial setting at the back of the stage. This appears first in *Eastward Ho*. Here is the direction at the beginning of the play:

> *Enter* Master Touchstone *and* Quicksilver *at several doors*; Quicksilver *with his hat, pumps, short sword and dagger, and a racket trussed up under his cloak. At the middle door, enter* Golding, *dis-*

> *covering a goldsmith's shop, and walking short turns before it.*
> (I.i.O.1-5)

This is surely an indication of a middle entry with some sort of a booth displayed. Act II begins with this:

> Touchstone, Golding *and* Mildred, *sitting on either side of the stall.*
> (II.i.O.1-2)

—manifestly a "discovery." We may note, too, that Touchstone spoke the last lines of Act I, which confirms the general belief that in the private theatres at this time there were intervals between the acts. But if Touchstone's stall is a prominent part of the scenic display in *Eastward Ho*, the tomb in *The Widow's Tears* is even more so. Yet here indeed we have to wonder whether "discoveries" were also not more frequently used. The play begins with this stage direction:

> Tharsalio *solus, with a glass in his hand, making ready.*

And in the second scene we have merely the names of Lysander and Lycus, with no *"Enter"* before them. So, too, at the beginning of Act II; and again the act begins with Tharsalio present, although he had left the stage at the end of Act I. The absence of an obvious entry is found also at the beginnings of Act II, Scene iii, Act II, Scene iv, and Act IV, Scene i. We must not pay too much attention to this, remembering that the classical method of heading scenes, preserved by Jonson and others before him, merely listed the names of characters who were to appear—and Chapman was indeed classically minded. But what does force itself on us in this play is the use of an approximation to masque-like staging: in the descent of Hymen—"*Music*: Hymen *descends, and six* Sylvans *enter beneath, with torches*" (III.ii.81.1-2)—we have a clear indication of two stage levels, and it is also made clear at line 108 —"O, would himself descend, and me command"—that Hymen actually descends only part of the way. What is even more evident is that the tomb, in which Cynthia and Ero plan at first to give themselves to death in mourning for Lysander, is a substantial structure. It is referred to in the opening stage direction to Act IV, Scene ii:

> *Enter* Lysander . . . *He discovers the tomb, looks in, and wonders, etc.*
> (IV.ii.O.1-3)

Soon Ero clearly opens a door or looks through a window
and addresses Lysander in reply to his "Ope, or I'll force
it open" (IV.ii.18). From the *"looks"* in the opening stage
direction, it is apparent that a window of some sort is there.
When the doors are open, both Cynthia and Ero are visible,
and ready to talk to Lysander. Later Ero *"shuts up the
tomb"* (IV.ii.179), and the first stage direction of Act IV,
Scene iii, includes *"the tomb opening"*; similarly, the conclud-
ing stage direction of Act IV is "S*he* [Ero] *shuts the tomb.*"
That it is possible to see into the shut tomb is again evident
in the stage direction (V.i.22.1): "Tharsalio *looking into the
tomb"*; and that it is glass that allows this is evident from his
following speech:

> 'Slight, who's here?
> A soldier with my sister! Wipe, wipe, see,
> Kissing, by Jove! She, as I lay, 'tis she! (V.i.22-4)

Soon after, we have *"The tomb opens"* (V.i.80.1), evidently,
as Parrott indicates, disclosing Lysander, Cynthia and Ero.
An equally evident "discovery" is found at the beginning of Act
V, Scene ii:

> *Tomb opens and* Lysander *within lies along*, Cynthia *and* Ero.

And at line 61 of this scene, Lysander "*Shut*[s] *the tomb*" and
comes forward to speak a soliloquy. Ero opens it again at line
146, and Tharsalio sees Cynthia's *"head laid on the coffin, etc."*
It is closed again at the end of this scene, opened again by Ero at
Act V, Scene iii, line 74, and we are told that here Tharsalio
"enters" it. Finally, at line 191, "Soldiers *thrust up* Lysander
from the tomb." Despite *"thrust up"*, I think it is evident that
the audience must see, and sometimes see into, the tomb from
Act IV, Scene ii, to the end of the play. We may, I think, deduce
that, when the tomb was open, a small footboard remained in
front. We are here concerned with a stage structure comparable
with Touchstone's shop in *Eastward Ho*, but a good deal more
elaborate. In addition, we should note that an upper level is

needed in the masque scene, and there is a stage direction "*going over the stage*" (I.ii.36.2), the possible significance of which has been drawn to our attention by Allardyce Nicoll.[15] What we may deduce, I think, from the plays discussed here, is that some sort of central structure, providing a third way of entry, was not unusual in the private theatres, and that an "above" was possible although not used many times within a single play.

The Widow's Tears is a sardonic piece of writing, showing how one widow was captivated by a brash young man who would not take no for an answer, and another, although determined to die in honour of her husband's memory, could not resist the advances of the man, actually her allegedly dead husband in disguise, who next presented himself to her. This may be what Professor Bradbrook calls "bitter comedy." Anyway, it is very good fun, a splendid re-telling of the Ephesian widow's story. It has two plots, but they fit together like those of *Eastward Ho*, unlike the sentimental and satiric stories of *Westward Ho*. Moreover, the Governor's judgment at the end seems to parody the giving of judgment in so many preceding plays—that of Henry V on Falstaff, that of the King of France on Bertram, that of Vincentio on Lucio and Angelo. It seems to anticipate the failure of Justice Overdo in *Bartholomew Fair*. The Elizabethans and Jacobeans were, perhaps, less taken in by the idea of law, as practised in their time, than some recent scholars have been. After all, Hooker—despite his admiration for the idea of law—never asserted that it was uniformly administered in the best way in his time.

I may perhaps be allowed to make one further observation. Sometimes I have been rebuked for exhibiting the human frailty of the Duchess of Malfi, and few criticisms of my writing have amused me more. She is surely the supreme widow in Renaissance drama. What Chapman and, for example, Middleton in *More Dissemblers Besides Women* demonstrate is that there was indeed a strong prejudice against remarriage, which could be dramatically presented as a joke at the widow's expense, as Chapman does it, or could be sententiously enunciated, as in the Middleton play. The great triumph of Webster's Duchess is that, despite the prejudice against remarriage

---

[15] "Passing over the Stage," *Shakespeare Survey 12* (1959), pp. 47-55.

Clifford Leech

and the belief in the comic vulnerability of widows, she securely wins both tragic stature and an honourable married state.[16] We should remind ourselves too that *The Duchess of Malfi* was played not only at the Globe but at Blackfriars.

[16] Cf. Gunnar Boklund, *The Duchess of Malfi: Sources, Themes, Characters* (Cambridge, Mass., 1962), pp. 95-96.

The Boar's Head Again

HERBERT BERRY

This is part two of my project about the public playhouse in the Boar's Head Inn, Whitechapel.[1] In the first part I tried to demonstrate that there was such a thing as a public playhouse in the Boar's Head, Whitechapel, that it was no less than the third house at the end of Elizabeth's reign—in importance probably, in legality certainly—built at much the same time as those other new houses, the Swan, the first Globe, the second Blackfriars, the Fortune, and the Red Bull. It was licensed next after the Globe and Henslowe's enterprises, and operated with what looks like success from 1598 until at least 1608. I tried to make this demonstration mostly by producing a tangle of lawsuits, dating from 1599 to 1603, over the ownership of the inn once the playhouse was built in it. Now, in my second part, I should like to explain some events leading up to the lawsuits, discuss some of the people concerned in them, and explain more closely than I could two years ago what the yard of the Boar's Head may have looked like and what happened to it in the years from then until now. At last, I shall propose where I think the Greater London Council should place their blue plaque.

In my first part, I showed that the Boar's Head Inn was a copyhold of the Manor of Stepney, owned in the 1580s by Ed-

[1] I read the first part at the First International Conference on Elizabethan Theatre, held at the University of Waterloo in July 1968. See "The Playhouse in the Boar's Head Inn, Whitechapel," *The Elizabethan Theatre* [I], ed. David Galloway (Toronto, 1969), pp. 45-73.

As with part one, I am indebted here to the Canada Council for grants which made most of the work possible. Transcripts of documents in the P.R.O. appear by permission of the Controller of H.M.S.O.

mund Poley[2] and, after his death, by his widow, Jane. She leased it in 1594 to Oliver Woodliffe, who agreed to build a playhouse in the place which (no doubt) the Poleys meant to acquire when the lease fell in. Eventually Woodliffe subleased most of the inn to Richard Samwell, and in 1598 and 1599 the two of them built the playhouse. Neither, however, could afford the money required, so in 1599 Samwell subleased his part to the actor, Robert Browne (leader of Derby's Men), and Woodliffe his part to the financier, Francis Langley (who had already built the Swan).

The Poleys and Woodliffes were representative types of Elizabethan bourgeois. The Poleys were the squires of Badley in Suffolk. In the 1560s, the squire was John. He had done well to marry, before 1548, Anne Wentworth, one of the sixteen children of Thomas Wentworth, whom Henry VIII made Lord Wentworth in 1529 and Edward VI enriched by the gift of the Manor of Stepney in 1550. The bishops of London had held the manor since before the conquest and had alienated it to the Crown only a few weeks before the Crown bestowed it on Wentworth. Like most property in Whitechapel, the Boar's Head was a copyhold of that manor. The appearance, then, of Anne Wentworth's brother-in-law (her husband's younger brother), Edmund Poley, in Whitechapel was probably not a coincidence. Moreover, one of her children, another Edmund, became steward of the manor in the next generation and a kind of secretary to the second and third lords Wentworth.[3] The Edmund Poley of the Boar's Head was uncle to the Edmund Poley, steward of the manor.

On January 14, 1562, at St. Mary Matfellon (the parish church of Whitechapel), the Edmund Poley who was to be of the Boar's Head married Jane, born Grove of White Walton in Berkshire, but then widow of John Tranfield of Whitechapel, who had died only two months before, and whose child she had borne only six months before. Poley must have been in his thirties, for he was apparently of age when his father (another Edmund) made his will in 1548 and died in 1549.[4] Whitechapel

---

[2] I spelled the name "Pooley" in part one because it was usually spelled that way; but the family seems consistently to have spelled it as "Poley."

[3] C.3/190/8; C.142/237/119; C.S.P., Dom., 1581-90, pp. 21, 74. This Edmund died in 1613, his will being P.C.C. 107 Capel. See part one, n. 10 and Stow, Survey of London (1598), pp. 405-06.

was then changing from a rural suburb to a thickly residential, commercial and manufacturing one. Stow described the process twice (pp. 92, 348). Tranfield bequeathed to his wife at least one potentially valuable tract there, a "greate garden plott." As a septuagenarian who had lived near the place for forty-seven years told the court of Chancery in 1591, a great part of it was in those days "a ver[i]e marrushe or wett grounde," and the rest "served (savinge reverence to this ho[norable] Courte) to no better use then to make a lay stall for the butchers inhabetinge thereabouts." It had only one building, an old "Shedd or Hovell." Poley, as we shall see, did better with it. It is tempting to guess that he acquired the Boar's Head in the same way and (as the map of c.1560 attributed to Ralph Agas suggests) in something like the same state.

The Poleys prospered. Their first child, a son, Henry, was born in December 1562. Other children followed in 1564, 1565 (John, baptised on October 28, who becomes important here), 1566, all baptised at St. Mary Matfellon, and one or two others. One or two were also buried there.[5] In 1572, the Poleys leased Tranfield's tract for £20 a year for twenty-one years to a gardener, John Myllian, who began a process of enriching the Poleys. Presumably he drained the garden, then planted root crops and built a house for himself at "greate cost." He sold his lease after five years, and others took up the work. Even though the lease had only sixteen years to run, presumably shrewd men built six more dwellings on the plot and divided the rest into at least thirty gardens, all well fenced, planted and trimmed, most with a garden house and some with tenters for use in the cloth trade. Myllian and the rest spent upwards of £500. Before long the lease was sublet for £36 a year and by the time it was ready to fall in on Lady Day (March 25), 1593, it was worth something like £67 a year.[6]

Before Edmund Poley could reap this harvest, however, he died. He was buried at St. Mary Matfellon on August 11, 1587, leaving his wife to claim his properties.[7] He left no will. His heir, Henry, may have been one of the "Englishmen of credit"

---

[4] Registers (G.L.C., P.93/MRY 1/1), I, 2^v, 3, 3^v, 20^v; Jane's will, P.C.C. 47 Woodhall; and Edmund Sr.'s will, P.C.C. 31 Populwell.
[5] Registers, I, 4^v, 6^v, 8^v, 9^v, 13 (2), and Jane's will.
[6] C.3/227/19; C.24/225 pt. II/1. One of the lessees was a clothworker, Henry Browne. His surname crops up frequently in the history of the Boar's Head.
[7] Guildhall, MSS. 9168/14, f. 232^v, and 9065^k, f. 167^v

living in Spain in 1595, but there were plenty of Poleys alive then and, because one of the squires of Badley had borne it, Henry was probably a common family name. The Boar's Head Henry had an uncle Henry who, if he was alive in 1595, was more likely to be an Englishman of credit. Besides, the Boar's Head Henry and his mother were living at the Boar's Head in 1594 when, the Myllian lease having just fallen in (and Jane a year or two before having forced the principal lessees to put the place in good repair), he and she leased the Boar's Head to Oliver Woodliffe with a view to its improvement, also for twenty-one years. Henry also lived in Whitechapel and was buried at St. Mary Matfellon on March 27, 1596.[8]

His brother, the new heir, John, was one of three John Poleys who had gone successfully to war. One, an old man and a professional soldier, had been knighted by Howard of Effingham in 1588. He was dead by 1607. Two others were knighted by Essex in Dublin in 1599, one who eventually married Abigail, a wealthy widow who survived him, and the other, now of the Boar's Head, apparently unmarried. Two years later, on June 20, 1601, his mother followed his father and brother into the burial registers of St. Mary Matfellon, leaving him the Whitechapel properties and the lawsuits over the lease of the Boar's Head.[9]

Sir John Poley of the Boar's Head did not mean, like his father, to be a magnate of Whitechapel. He began amassing an estate near his landed cousins in Suffolk, especially at Columbine Hall. So when the lease of the Boar's Head fell in 1616, the place was for sale. But first he married, probably in 1613, at about forty-eight years of age, an Ursula, who by 1628 had borne him two sons and six daughters, all baptised in Suffolk, his heir being John (1621) and his second son, Edmund (1628). Poley was not hugely wealthy. He could give his daughters portions of only £200 each, and his executors had trouble raising that.[10]

[8] H.M.C., *Salisbury*, V, 357; Registers, I, 36. The uncle was apparently younger than the Boar's Head Henry's father (P.C.C. 31 Populwell).
[9] C.24/331 (Pooley v. Beecher); C.2/Chas.I/L.59/54; /T.48/67; Registers I, 46. Abigail's maiden name was Wikes; her first husband was John Worsley and her second Richard Luther.
[10] In about 1603 he was taxed in Whitechapel, where he gave his goods as worth £20; most of his neighbours gave £3 or £4; his mother had twice given £6; but some men in Whitechapel gave £40. One of his daughters died in 1636. His wife

Woodliffe was a different matter. He was of meaner origin and proceeded by meaner tracks. Apparently he was made free of the Haberdashers' Company in May 1572, but he did not become a citizen of London like the princes of the London companies. Along with many others, he was and remained yeoman of his company: of the livery, but one of the "manufacturing small masters" rather than one of the merchants who ruled the company.[11] He made his way, like many others, by lending money to hard cases at the going rates, 8 per cent or 10 per cent or better, and then vigorously achieving repayment. He and others, for example, lent money to a Gloucestershire man, Henry Dante, from Simondsales Down near Dursley. When Dante did not repay, they took him to court and got the inevitable "executions," Woodliffe's for £106. But Dante was in Gloucestershire, surrounded by friends and neighbours. Woodliffe and the others, therefore, undertook to propel the law at a more determined pace than it was likely to go on its own. With Woodliffe and a servant among them, they set out for Gloucestershire. They persuaded the sheriff and a deputy to arrest Dante and they proposed to help. Woodliffe armed himself with pistols, according to Dante, a dagger without a case by his own admission, and he equipped his servant with sword and buckler. If one is reminded of the man of La Mancha, it is as well. The company arrived at Simondsales Down on May 25, 1582. Dante's neighbours cheerfully rallied to defend him from both the law and strangers. Pitched battles followed that day and the next. It seems that Dante and his friends won, and to protect that dangerous triumph, Dante went to the Star Chamber to charge Woodliffe and the others with making an affray. Woodliffe, he said, was "A man of smale conscyence & of harde dealinge" who "Rydeth & goethe about the Countrey wth a case of Pystolles," and he added, for the benefit of the court which made a specialty of guarding the Queen's peace, "to the great evell exampell of

was dead by 1657. E.179/142/234 (m.3'), 239, 254; C.2/Chas.I/P.90/54; C.54/3597/m.38-41.
[11] He is given in the lawsuits as free of that company. In his marriage licence he gave himself as yeoman and in his admon. act his widow gave him as of the Diocese of London rather than as citizen of London. The name appears only once in the "Freedoms" book of the company, 1526-1614, spelled "Woodclief" in the entry, "Woodlief" in the index. His master was Edward Slatier. See Wm. F. Kahl, *The Guilds and Companies of London* (London, 1963), p. 231.

Herbert Berry

others." For his part, Woodliffe assured the court that Dante was "a very dysperat & Leowde man."[12]

Twelve years late, Woodliffe tried a surer route to substance. He married, in January 1594, Susan Chaplyn, widow of John Chaplyn of St. Katherine Cree, a man of means and a citizen of London. Chaplyn had died without a will in July 1592, and she had got the administration of his considerable goods.[13] Not coincidentally, probably, some ten months after his marriage, Woodliffe took his lease on the Boar's Head and planned to erect a theatrical enterprise there. He probably also moved his ménage into the place, where they joined Jane Poley and her son Henry, for the Woodliffes' names commence joining the others in the registers of St. Mary Matfellon, and they were certainly living in the inn in 1599. A son, Oliver, was baptised at St. Mary Matfellon on April 19, 1595, and in May 1597, a Susan Chaplyn, presumably a daughter of Woodliffe's wife, married Phillip Pound there.[14] Perhaps Woodliffe's wife had been married to Chaplyn more than a summer or two.

That other city man in the Boar's Head, Francis Langley, the draper, began at the opposite end of the city scale. Yet when the two launched themselves into the playhouse business in 1594, Langley with the Swan and Woodliffe with the Boar's Head, Langley was on his way to a bankruptcy, which the playhouses helped to cause, and Woodliffe to a competency, which the playhouses probably did little to advance. From 1599 Langley suffered one judgment after another against him in the courts of common law—three in 1599, one in 1600, two in 1601, amounting in all to £1,441.8.0d. (not counting Woodliffe's judgment), the last being for £610 brought by his brother-in-law Ashley. After Langley died in July 1602, Ashley did his best to squeeze the money out of his sister, Langley's widow. But if Woodliffe suffered one pursuer to get a judgment against him for £30.10.0d. in 1601, he beat off another in the same year who sought a judgment for £60. When he sued

[12] St.Ch.5/D.36/9.
[13] The bond she had to post on July 18 to get the administration of his goods was £77 5s. 1d., the seond highest of the month in the London Commissary Court (Guildhall, MS.9168/14, f.240ᵛ). The marriage licence is in *Allegations for Marriage Licences Issued by the Bishop of London, 1520-1610*, p. 212. Woodliffe gave himself as of Barking in Essex and her as of Eastham in Essex. He did not know her husband's Christian name.
[14] C.P.40/1655/m.724; Registers, I, 34ᵛ, 39ᵛ.

38

the Langleys for the first of their bonds in 1602, he got a judgment for £107.10.0d. because the Langleys stopped appearing
in court against him. He tried to exact the money out of Richard
Langley's goods twice in 1602 and twice in 1603. The actor
Browne, however, or perhaps Browne's mentor, Israel Jordan,
drove Woodliffe, in 1603, to appeal to equity in the Court of
Requests. Woodliffe had failed to convince Common Pleas
that it was only because of threats to life and limb that he gave
Browne a by now unpaid bond. The sum involved, however,
was only £16.[15]

Langley's effort to chase the actor Robert Browne and his
company (Lord Derby's) out of the Boar's Head was also
abortive, even though he had Woodliffe's bonded promise
of help and Susan Woodliffe's active help. On December 15,
1599, he had subleased to his creature, Thomas Wollaston,
who, on the same day, subleased to his other creature, Richard
Bishop, the part of the yard on which stood the posts which
held up Browne's galleries. Hence, Langley insisted, not only
that part of the yard, but the galleries above it, belonged to
Bishop. Browne and the Samwells argued that the yard belonged
to them and refused to pay Bishop rent. Langley harassed the
Samwells unmercifully in the Marshalsea Court, but Browne
apparently continued playing. When, in April 1600, the Samwells escalated their defence to the Star Chamber, Langley
escalated his harassment to the Queen's Bench and made
Browne his target, but again, apparently, without much disturbing Browne's theatrical enterprises. On May 20, 1600,
perhaps Browne and the carpenter who had built the playhouse, John Mago, were altering the position of some of the
fixed posts which held up the galleries and so affecting the
fixed seats in those galleries. Bishop, in any event, repaired
to the Queen's Bench to charge them with breaking and
entering his premises, throwing down the fixed posts and
seats, and making mayhem to the value of £5. He also charged
them with carrying away the seats and doing other enor-
mities against the Queen's peace to the value of £20.[16]

---

[15] C.54/1034; K.B.27/1358/m.518^v; /1360/m.1057^v; /1361/m.536, 557^v; /1367/m.
525; /1369/m.872, 876^v; /1370/m.375^v; /1376/m.279^v. And C.P.40/1655/m.724;
/1693/m.1514^v; /1701/m.109.

[16] K.B.27/1364/m.259; /1367/m.199^v. The Latin runs, "quosdum postes & sedes
in domo predicta fixas tunc ibidem deieceruntur & prostrauerantur &
maheremurentur euisdem domus ad valenciam centum solidorum," etc. The

Browne remained in possession of the Boar's Head and continued to refuse to pay Bishop rent for the use of the yard, which Bishop's £20 may represent. But Browne and Mago had to bond themselves to appear when the case should come up. On October 9, they pleaded not guilty. On October 22, Bishop pressed the charges, and on November 21, although the case arrived before Sir John Popham, Chief Justice of the Queen's Bench, Bishop did not. So Popham released Browne and Mago and ordered Bishop to be charged with making a false claim. Bishop returned to Queen's Bench the next spring (1601) to reopen the case. He charged additionally that Browne and Mago had expelled him from his premises. Browne and Mago again pleaded not guilty (on May 20) and demanded a trial. But this time Bishop did not press his charges and so the case did not go for trial. It simply disappeared, and Browne continued in effective charge of the Boar's Head.

The death of Richard Samwell the elder in the winter of 1600-1 probably inhibited the growth of these lawsuits. That of Langley in July 1602, surely deprived them of bravura. But it was the great plague of 1603 which ended them altogether, as it ended as well playing at the Boar's Head and everywhere else in London for months. Woodliffe was the first to go. He was buried with no fewer than twenty-seven others at St. Mary Matfellon on July 30. It was one of the worst days. A Susan Samwell was buried there on August 26. Browne was buried there on October 16, when the plague had nearly run its course; he was one of only three on that day.[17] Like Chaplyn and Langley, Browne and Woodliffe died without wills—perhaps death took them all by surprise—so Susan Browne applied to the Prerogative Court of Canterbury, and Susan Woodliffe a second time to the London Commissary Court for the administration of husbands' goods. Susan Woodliffe got hers on August 26, and Susan Browne hers on January 9, 1604. Both ladies no doubt inherited their husbands' interest in the Boar's Head. Susan Woodliffe posted a bond which was about a twenty-eighth of that she had posted for Chaplyn. Seven months later she married James Vaughan at St. Mary Matfellon.[18]

seats could have been in the yard, of course, but Woodliffe mentioned seats in galleries (see *Elizabethan Theatre* [I], p. 52).

[17] Registers, I, 51, 53, 54.

[18] MS. 9168/15, f. 246 (Woodliffe's bond was 57s. 4d.); PROB/6/6, f. 183; Registers, I, 48.

Some notes, finally, about the residents of the Boar's Head. The child Winifred Samwell had at breast when Langley had her carried off by the Marshalsea tipstaffs on Christmas Eve, 1599, was Rebecca, some six weeks old (though her outraged grandfather said three), baptised at St. Mary Matfellon on November 11. Winifred was the wife of the younger Richard Samwell. She bore another child baptised there, Sara, on February 24, 1601.[19] When Browne was taxed in Whitechapel in 1600, he gave his goods as worth £4, a sum many residents there gave. His wife bore him three children during their four years at the Boar's Head: William (who became a player and can now be added to the handful for whom we have a year of birth), baptised April 25, 1602; Elizabeth, baptised February 13, 1603; and Anne, born posthumously, baptised January 22, 1604.[20] On February 8, 1603, there were long stretches of broken pavement in the Queen's highway in Whitechapel to the injury of pedestrians. One of them, 165′ by 16′6″, was adjacent to lands which Robert Browne, "Stage player," held, presumably the Boar's Head. County officials took him and two others to court to make them repair their portions, and Browne or his widow satisfied the court by April 1604.[21] The only public thoroughfare of that length adjacent to the Boar's Head was, in 1676, the alley just east of the long building in the inn. The frontage of the inn on Whitechapel must have been considerably shorter, and it seems likely that the inn had no frontage on Hog Lane. In any case, Browne seems still to be in charge of the Boar's Head in 1603, when all the lawsuits were coming to an end.

II

Browne's sublease of the Boar's Head fell in at Christmas, 1615, and Woodliffe's lease on Lady Day following. Probably the

---

[19] Registers, I, 43ᵛ, 45ᵛ.

[20] E.179/142/234, m.4; Registers, I, 47ᵛ, 48ᵛ, 49ᵛ. Their stepfather, Green, mentioned them all in his will in 1612 (G.L.C., 129 Hamer). See also Chambers, *Elizabethan Stage*, II, 237-38, and Bentley, *Jacobean and Caroline Stage*, II, 391-92.

[21] K.B.29/242/m.54ᵛ, 55, 55ᵛ. The word used for Browne's dimensions is "virgata." He has ten of them by one. The word can mean either "yard" or "virgate," that is, a rod. Usually it meant yard when used for such things as cloth, but rod when used for land. By a statute of 35 Eliz., a rod was 16′6″. See *N.E.D.*, "Yard," sb.², 8-10; Eric Partridge, *Origins* (London, 1966), "Verge," 2; "Yard," 2.

playhouse ended then, if it had not before. Poley seems to have sold a strip down the middle of the great yard to Samuel Rowley without much delay. Because Poley held the whole place by copyhold of the manor of Stepney, he passed this strip as a copyhold. Then he enfranchised the rest of the inn on June 23, 1618; that is, he paid the manor to give up its claims on the property so that he and his successors could own it by free socage and no longer have to pay fees to the manor for every transaction concerning it. He had decided that it was more profitable to sell it in relatively small pieces and that these pieces were more saleable as freeholds. The manor, however, continued to exact from him and his successors a small annual rent of 16d. for the Boar's Head. The Rowley piece, of course, continued as a copyhold.

Poley looked for buyers among people who already held properties in or around the Boar's Head. On December 20, 1621, he confirmed two such sales on the Close Roll: one to Thomas Needler, citizen and merchant of London, who paid £120, and the other to William Browne, citizen and cooper of London, who paid £200. Needler's rent to the manor was to be 2d. a year and Browne's 4d., so that presumably the sales comprised three-eighths of the Boar's Head.[22] Both entries on the Close Roll are full copies of the deeds which Poley and his purchasers agreed to. Poley and Browne said specifically that the stage and tiring house no longer existed and that two buildings on the site had been pulled down for rebuilding "in a better forme." So by December 1621, at the very latest, the Boar's Head playhouse was no more, and the Boar's Head itself was rapidly becoming a tangle of small holdings, an enclave off Whitechapel in which people lived, shopped (Browne's deed mentions shops and a butcher who lived adjacent to Browne's part of the yard), and eventually even worshipped (in the first half of the eighteenth century an independent meeting-house stood, perhaps uneasily, on part of the site of the tiring house and stage).[23] By 1621 the name Boar's Head was already an anachronism.

[22] C.54/2515/11; /2471/17. Needler and Browne seem to have had Poley levy a fine for the enfranchisement: C.P.25(2)/324/Hil.19 Jas. I/10. Needler called himself "Nedle alias Needler" in 1621, but he and his family used "Needler" afterwards.

[23] The land tax returns for 1734 and 1746 (Guildhall, MSS. 6015/2, 15) and the Rocque map (1746).

By the time Poley died at sixty-nine years of age, on February
13 or 14, 1635, he had sold the rest of the Boar's Head,[24] but I
have not been able to trace any of the sales, much less find
another deed. Nor have I been able to find any other deeds until
modern times. The evidence about what was in the Boar's
Head yard in Elizabethan times, therefore, consists mainly of
allusions in lawsuits, official copies of two deeds belonging
to late 1621, and maps.

No map before the fire of 1666 is even remotely reliable
for the suburbs east of the city. Because of the fire, the city
engaged a group of surveyors to make the first accurate
plan. It was finished quickly; by December 1666, the men's
work had been brought together into one map by John Leake.
This map was not published and is probably lost, but Wenceslaus
Hollar made a picture map from it which was printed in 1667.[25]
The Boar's Head was not burned in the fire, and appears at the
right hand edge of the map, forty-five years after the deeds.

The fire soon produced another and much better map, the
Ogilby and Morgan one, printed in 1676. It is incomparably
the best map of London, at least until Horwood's in the
1790s. Its authors tried to show not just every street and lane,
but every yard and every building, every property line and
even important divisions of buildings. Their scale was huge—
100' to the inch. They took elaborate pains to get their measurements and angles right. But they did their work when surveying was in its infancy and when the deeds of 1621 were upwards of fifty-five years old. In a rapidly developing place
like Whitechapel, that is a lot. Moreover, by dividing the
scale bar on their map into tenths of an inch, Ogilby and
Morgan may have suggested that we depend on them only
down to ten feet. Nearly all the property lines, buildings,
and passages mentioned in Browne's deed, however, are
where one would expect to find them on the map, and dimen-

[24] His daughter Elizabeth gave the earlier date in a lawsuit about his property
(C.2/Chas.I/P.90/54); his I.P.M. gives the other (C.142/546/481/118). Neither
document mentions property in Whitechapel. He may have sold his parents' great
garden plot to John Wood and Anne, his wife, in 1632. If so, it then had on it two
messuages, 14 cottages, and a quarter acre of land (C.P.25(2)/457/Hil. 7 Chas.
I/19).
[25] Ida Darlington and James Howgego, *Printed Maps of London circa 1553-1850*
(London, 1964), #21. I am indebted to Mr. Howgego for advice about early maps
of London.

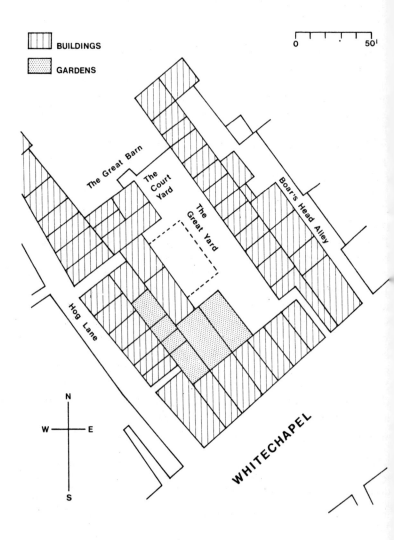

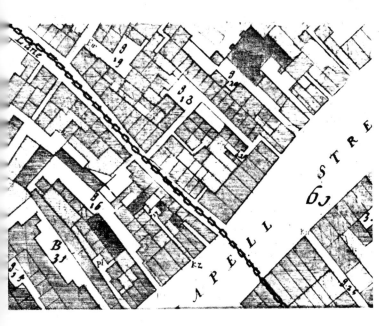

The Boar's Head from Ogilby and Morgan's map of London, 1676. *Reproduced by kind permission of the Greater London Council.*

B 31: Blue Boar Inn	g 18: Boar's Head Yard
g 14: Black Bull Alley	g 19: Tripe Yard
g 15: Parrot Alley	g 20: Boar's Head Alley
g 16: White Horse Alley	g 25: Irish Court
g 17: Anchor and Hart Alley	h 79: Harrow Alley

sions are not much different. What survived around the Boar's Head until the first large-scale Ordnance Survey maps, like the little which survives still, was and is also close to Ogilby and Morgan. It even seems that in measurements around the Boar's Head between points which their chainmen would have found obvious and accessible, Ogilby and Morgan were generally out no more than 3 per cent to 4 per cent and usually less. Between concealed or inaccessible points, probably they could be out somewhat more. (In what follows I have put an asterisk after such dimensions. Please see the appendix.)

So with a decent caveat, here is Ogilby and Morgan—and following are the deeds.

First let us dispose of the Needler one. I suspect that the property it describes lay in the north or northeast end of the Boar's Head, well away from the playhouse. The description of the property at the beginning of the deed, unluckily, makes Thorpe's remarks before Shakespeare's Sonnets seem a piece of simple lucidity. Needler bought

> All those foure tenements scituate in the parishe of St Mary Matfellon alias Whitechaple in the County of Midd Wherein now one Elizabeth Browne widow Robert Stamford John Florey & one Robert Lockdale now dwell with certeine other buildings sometymes called a stable & the chamber over it to the same adioyning & a place of ground adioyning being parcell of the buildings & yard of the Boares head as they doe lye in the said parish against the garden late in thoccupacion of one John Needler towards the north & conteyne in length from the end of the great barne parcell of the said Boares head vnto the outside of the corner post of the same range of buildings forty five foote & five ynches of assize & on the south side from the outside of the crosse buildings by the mayne post & the yard in right range against the Court yard measured out thirty nyne foote in length & thirty foure foote in breadth south to the post of the said great barne forty seaven foote six ynches against the Court yard & in breadth at both ends east & west thirty eight foote of assize.

Needler mortgaged property in the Boar's Head in 1632. If it was the same as that of the deed, five tenements had grown to eight. In the mortgage, the property is "Eight mesuags or tenements now in thoccupacion of the said Thomas [Needler] . . . in or neere a Courte ground or place commonly called the Boares Head." Needler died in 1650, still unable to redeem the property. His widow could not even continue to make payments on the mortgage, so the property left the family. His son and grandson sued to get it back in 1658 and 1659 because they thought it then worth more to sell than was owing on the mortgage.[26] In these lawsuits, the property is repeatedly eight houses in Boar's Head Alley, presumably that passage shown in Ogilby and Morgan behind (east of) the long building.

---

[26] C.54/2947/24; C.7/250/33; /545/25; C.24/840, pt. II/9.

One reason for putting Needler's property in the northern part of the inn is that in the deed it is partly bound by the great barn, which is there in the lawsuits. Another is that in both deed and mortgage it is also partly bound by the "court" yard held in common by the residents of the Boar's Head. The only part of the yard of the inn which was kept open and public after the deeds of 1621, indeed until the latter part of the nineteenth century, was the northern end of the main yard. This yard may have been called "court" to distinguish it from the great yard south of it. Such a distinction is in the deed of 1594 (as reported in the lawsuits of 1600), where a "backe yarde" is different from "the greate yarde."[27] Because Samwell had the right "to lay dunge in" the back yard, it may have been near the great barn, as the court yard was. Possibly, then, the two were the same, and "court" merely a euphemism for "backe." I do not know what the rest of Needler's description means.

Fortunately, Browne's property included the plot on which the stage and tiring house stood, and so his deed takes us ultimately to the shape of the playhouse, the location of the stage, and a dimension. The Boar's Head is only the second Elizabethan playhouse for which we have so much (its near contemporary and rival on the north bank, the Fortune, is the other).

The description of the property in Browne's deed is simpler than in Needler's, but it is not so explicit as one would like either. Browne bought

All those severall roomes & dwelling places parcell of a capitall messuage or tenemente comonly called or knowne by the name of the Boares head as the[y] now be or late were in the severall possessions of Elizabeth Mitchell widowe John younge John Price William Bowyer Thomas Gawen Nicholas Jones together with one roome called a chamber roome builded over the tenemente wherein the said Elizabeth Mitchell now dwelleth now or late in the possession of Roger Meggs together alsoe with one roome late in the occupacion of one Francis Pleyvie together alsoe with soe much of the said Boares head yard in measure as by measure & platt were

[27] St.Ch.5/S.74/3, the bill and the Woodliffes' reply. When the deed is formally explained at the beginning of the bill, the "great yard" is just that, but the other is "one garden and Backyarde occupyed and vsed to and w th the said messuage [i.e., the Boar's Head] together w th the wayes and passages occupyed w th the said garden and yarde."

lately sett out & measured from the south side of the roome in the occupacion of the said Elizabeth Mitchell right downe into the said Boares head yard to a stake there sett upp & conteyneth by estimacion fiftie & three foote of assize and in bredth from the said stake unto the yard or garden of the said William Browne at the north end from the east unto the west twenty twoe foote & five ynches together alsoe with soe much of the said Boares head ground As lately was builded & knowne for a tyreing house or Stage & twoe tenements late in the severall occupacions of humphrey Plevy & John Walford and have ben lately pulled downe to be reedified and builded in a better forme as the same by measure doe contayne at the north end next the tenemente wherein Thomas Milles butcher now dwelleth in breadth from the pale belonging to the Coppyhold tenements of Samuell Rowley west to the corner of the said tenements wherein the said Thomas Milles now dwelleth thirty six foote & a halfe of assize & in breadth at the south end next the garden of the said William Browne the like assize of thirty six foote & a halfe & doe contayne on the east & west side thereof thirty nyne foote & seaven ynches.

William Browne owned more property in Whitechapel than that in the Boar's Head. He had some copyhold lands which he passed to legatees in 1630 and a messuage which probably stood on the north side of Whitechapel, in Ogilby and Morgan the fourth house from the corner of Hog Lane. Its garden stretched back into the Boar's Head and (as the deed of 1621 reads) adjoined part of his purchase there. He wrote his will in 1633, "sicke in body by reason of age," where he described his part of the Boar's Head as "my said lands Tenem[ts] and houses in the Boars head yard in the parrish of White Chapell." They must have been worth at least the £10 to £12 a year, which he directed his successors to pay annually from them to various legatees. He died a year later, leaving his freehold properties in Whitechapel to his nephew, John Browne, who sold them in 1637—those in the Boar's Head, now described as one messuage (his part of the long building?) and nine cottages (his structures in the great yard?), to Robert Dixon and Humphrey Browne, and the messuage and garden probably adjoining them to Thomas Abraham.[28]

Browne was probably buying six divisions of the long

[28] Guildhall, MS. 9172/42, June 20, 1634 (Browne's will); C.P.25(2)/457/Easter 13 Chas. I/3, 19.

building and, except for Rowley's strip, the yard which lay before five of them. He was buying, that is, most of the great yard, which consisted now of a big plot west of Rowley's strip and a thin piece (about 8′ in Ogilby and Morgan) between Rowley's strip and the long building. He must have wanted the thin piece for access to his parts of the long building; it continued to be used so until the latter half of the nineteenth century. He wanted the big plot so that he could put up the nine cottages his nephew sold in 1637, or the eight premises (two of them not built over) shown in Ogilby and Morgan. Rowley's strip must have been the fenced-in rectangle which Ogilby and Morgan show in front of the long building.

The boundary of Browne's purchase in the yard would have run from the southern edge of the court yard (approximately marked in Ogilby and Morgan by the southern line of the widow Mitchell's premises) south along the front of the long building to a stake opposite the northern edge of Browne's garden, 53′ in the deed and about 55′3″* in Ogilby and Morgan.[29] His boundary then ran west across the open yard from the long building to the northern edge of his garden, 22′5″ in the deed, about a foot* less in Ogilby and Morgan. The boundary continued west along his garden to the eastern edge of the alley shown in Ogilby and Morgan, 36′6″ in the deed, about 9″* more in Ogilby and Morgan (the south line of the big plot). Browne's boundary then followed the alley north to the bigger alley running east from Hog Lane, 39′7″ in the deed, about two feet more in Ogilby and Morgan (the west line of the big plot). The boundary next followed the big alley east to Rowley's strip (the north line of the big plot), 36′6″ in the deed, about 36′2″* in the map. Presumably the boundary finished by running 22′5″ (22′3″* in Ogilby and Morgan) across the yard to the long building. The east line of the big plot ran along Rowley's strip to Browne's garden, 39′7″ in the deed, about a foot and a half more in the map.

Browne's big plot in the great yard had contained the two buildings recently pulled down for rebuilding in a better form, and the tiring house and stage. How the two buildings related to the tiring house and stage, the deed does not make

---

[29] If the widow Mitchell's boundary were 2′ to 3′ farther south, it would have been a better mark for the southern line of the court yard as well as in keeping with the measurement in the deed.

clear. The language of the deed suggests that the man who wrote it knew that two buildings, a tiring house, and a stage belonged to one scheme, but that he did not know how or did not think it worth the trouble to explain how. By using "or" rather than "and" between "tiring house" and "stage," he combined those two, both long defunct anyway, and he put separately the two more important structures, recently useful and soon to be useful again. What he wrote was sufficiently meaningful in 1621, but it would have been dangerously confusing twenty years before. He should have made the tiring house and stage as separate in the deed as they are in the leases and lawsuits written while they stood, [30] and, I suggest, he should have combined the two demolished buildings and the tiring house. For it must be a sound guess that those two buildings were two or more of Woodliffe's "certeyne Romes" on the western side of the yard on which he agreed to have his builders work, as well as on the tiring house, stage and gallery over the stage. Woodliffe's gallery over the stage must have run along the upper part of them, and the three feet of the yard he had in which to enlarge them must have been the distance he and the Poleys planned that the gallery should extend from the buildings. In the rebuilding of 1599 he probably added four feet. He could then have boxed in the space under his gallery and used that for his tiring house, or that plus part of the two buildings. In 1603, when he had finished all his building, the whole structure would have been what he described as "the Larder the Larder parler the well parler the Cole house the oate loaft the Tireing house & stage." He omitted here his gallery, which he had certainly built over the stage, because for the moment it was not legally relevant.

Needler's and Browne's deeds shared many clauses. Both men saw to it that Poley guaranteed them against the kind of trouble Samwell and Browne had had with Poley's mother's and brother's lease. Both men had specific use of the various parts of the inn which all inhabitants held in common—the pump, which was on Needler's property, a watercourse used for carrying away waste, which ran through Needler's property and had its "sink" in the garden of John Needler to the

---

[30] Perhaps one may use the word to support Dr. Hotson's suggestion that the tiring house was under the stage in general and at the Boar's Head in particular.

north, and a piece of "waste ground," 39' north and south by
34' east and west, which lay somewhere in the inn. More important, both deeds mention alleys, Needler's twice and
Browne's three times.

Needler's deed gave him the right to pass and repass "with
carte and carriage" from the buildings he was buying through
the "Court or common yard of the said Boares head by & through
a passage way of eight foote in widenesse to be made leading
from the said Court yard west into the common way or streete
called hoggelane." Later the deed repeated that Needler could
use "the said way unto or from the bargained premisses into &
from hogge lane aforesaid" forever. This alley, then, was
to be built *west* from the yard (specifically the "court" yard,
which seems to have been the northern part of the whole yard)
to Hog Lane, and it did not exist when the playhouse did. Such
an alley was built, is clearly shown in Ogilby and Morgan,
and remained in public use until 1964. In Ogilby and Morgan
it is about 8' wide. In the Ordnance Survey map of 1848-50 it
begins at about 9'6" and narrows to about 7'4".

Browne's deed is different. For one thing, he was to build an
alley and maintain it. For another, it is probably a different alley.
After the main description of the property, his deed provides,
"Except & alwaies reserved out of this bargaine & sale one
passage way of the breadth of eight foote & from the ground
the altitude of nyne foote to be made laid out & mayneteined
passageable by the said William Browne . . . in & through the
said parcell of ground where the stage was builte right discending from the way alonge out of hogge lane to be made of equall
breadth into the said Boares head yard with free passage for
the said Sir John Poley . . . and all other inhabitants in the said
Boares head yard with free passage there into or out from the
said Boares head yard by the said passage into hogge lane
aforesaid" forever. Later in the deed, Poley promised that
Browne should "enioy free & quiett passage . . . into and
through the said way unto & from the bargained premisses
into & from hogge lane afore said" forever. Finally, Browne
agreed that Poley and all his tenants should "have quiett &
free passage in the said passage way" and that Browne should
maintain it "passageable in such latitude & altitude as is afore-
mencioned & excepted" forever "for the use & benefitt of the
said Sir John Poley his heires & assignes or other Tenants &

Inhabitants in the buildings now or late parcell of the said Boares head which shall have their passage way thereby assigned lymitted or appointed by the said Sir John Poley."

The first provision suggests that the eight feet of the projected alley belonged to the plot on which the stage and tiring house stood, but was not counted in Browne's dimensions. Because this alley was to be "right discending" into the yard (not the court yard) from a "way" which already existed into Hog Lane, it must have run, unlike Needler's alley, from north to south (the dimension from the widow Mitchell's premises "right downe into" the yard also ran from north to south) and into the central part of the great yard. Because Browne had to build and maintain the alley, presumably he had the right to build over it. Hence Poley specified how high the alley had to be, and hence he and Browne did not intend that the alley should be a main thoroughfare. The second provision, like the final "with" phrase of the first, refers to the alley into Hog Lane and not Browne's. The third provision specified that Browne's alley was mainly for Browne's and Poley's use, and, despite the remark in the first clause about all other inhabitants of the yard, that the alley was not to be entirely public, unlike Needler's.

Browne's alley was also built and is also clearly shown in Ogilby and Morgan. It runs from Needler's alley down the west side of Browne's big plot, and at the bottom it turns east for a few feet into that plot, where it served both the south side of the plot and the north side of Browne's garden. Either Browne did not build it the full width that he and Poley had specified in the deed (perhaps because there was not land enough in the great yard), or by the time of Ogilby and Morgan it had been encroached along its full length, or Ogilby and Morgan are wrong about its width. Browne promised to build it 8' wide, but in the map it is only 4'. It disappeared in the eighteenth century.

III

We can make some shrewd guesses, then, about what the Boar's Head was like before the building of the playhouse in 1598 and 1599. We can be surer of what much of the playhouse looked like, and we can be nearly positive of some of the important ways in which the inn changed later.

In the 1590s, the inn did not occupy the corner of Hog Lane and Whitechapel, but the land behind the buildings standing around that corner. It had its main entry on Whitechapel, at the L-shaped extremity of the long building shown in Ogilby and Morgan. That extremity is said to belong to the inn in the lawsuits, and so are the three premises on Whitechapel across the entry from it, which were a hall, a parlour, and a kitchen, with chambers above them. A chamber belonging to the inn was also over the entry. The premises to the west of these on Whitechapel probably did not belong to the inn, nor did the gardens stretching behind them, whose fences probably marked the southern boundary of the great yard. The first of these premises was Browne's. The inn also had an entry into Hog Lane, but according to the suggestion in Needler's deed, it ran only to the back of the buildings (and a garden in the lawsuits) which stood along the western side of the great yard. Along most of the inn's eastern boundary stood the long building. In the north there was a smaller yard, the "court," or "backe" yard, surrounded on the south by the great yard, on the east by the long building, on the north by the great barn and perhaps another yard, and on the west perhaps by the hostry and the premises in which the Poleys lived.

The yard was, in effect, three adjacent yards all bound on the east by the straight line of the long building—a small one in the north probably called the court yard, a rather similar small one in the south, and the great yard in the middle. In Ogilby and Morgan, the northern yard is about 30′ square, the southern one about 34′8″° along the long building by about 27′9″ east and west. The great one is about 57′8″° along the long building by about 63′ to the western edge of the property, 43′6″° to the buildings in the west, which in 1676 replaced those recently demolished in 1621. The combined yard, then, stretched some 122′ north and south along the long building, was about 30′ across at its extremities, and bulged to half as much again at its middle. Other inns in Whitechapel had yards of similar shape, like the Blue Boar, but in Ogilby and Morgan, at least, their dimensions at the extremities and middle were much less.

It is obvious, then, why the Poleys and Woodliffe thought of plays. The open part of the inn was sizeable, and the great yard in the middle was big enough for an Elizabethan stage. Besides, the balcony along the long building suggested theatrical galleries. It is obvious, too, why Woodliffe did not put his stage at the north or south extremity of the yard. At either, the yard was too narrow for an Elizabethan stage, much less for the usual arrangement of stage surrounded by ground-lings at left and right as well as front. Moreover, had Woodliffe put his stage at either extremity, many customers would have been as much as a hundred feet away. Where he did put his stage, nobody could have been much more than forty feet away.

It is also obvious why Woodliffe put the stage out in the yard in 1598 and moved it six feet westwards when he and Samwell extended the galleries three to four feet in 1599. If the stage were out in the yard, persons in the north and south extremities could see it. The space between the front of the stage and the edge of the gallery along the long building, however, would have been so small (about 12′5″* if Ogilby and Morgan are right, and if the gallery was about 3′ deep) that when they extended the gallery the posts holding it up would have been very close to the front of the stage, and persons in the back of the extended gallery would not have been able to see the stage. So Woodliffe and Samwell gave up the sightlines of some persons in the corners of the yard in order to get more persons in the galleries.

The stage and tiring house occupied the western three-quarters of the great yard. From 1599 the plot containing them was (according to Browne's deed) 39′7″ on the east and west sides by 36′6″ on the north and south sides without the width of Browne's alley, 44′6″ with it. This plot protruded beyond the western line of the northern yard by about 8′6″ in Ogilby and Morgan and beyond the western line of the southern yard by somewhat less. This protrusion represents the front of the stage. Between it and the long building lay about 22′ of the great yard (in Ogilby and Morgan) for groundlings. Overhead for about six of the 22′ was the eastern gallery running along the long building. At the northern edge of the plot was the 8′ of open space (for groundlings, no doubt) which eventually became Needler's alley. Over at least part of the length of this strip was the northern gallery, probably about 6′ deep from 1599. At the southern edge of the stage plot in 1621 and in Ogilby and Morgan was the garden of Browne's house on Whitechapel. In 1599 there could have been 8′* or so for groundlings and a gallery overhead, as on the northern side, because in the map the back line of that garden extends about that much farther into the yard of the Boar's Head than the back line of the neighbouring garden; Browne might have bought that much before the deed of 1621, or even silently in that deed.

The eastern side of this plot represents the full width of the stage, 39'7". The only Elizabethan stage for which we have a similar dimension, that of the Fortune, was 43' wide. The depth of the Boar's Head stage is not so certain. The two buildings shown in Ogilby and Morgan at the back (western end) of the plot are about 15'° deep. If the two demolished buildings of Browne's deed were so deep and if one adds 7' for Woodliffe's gallery over the stage, one has left about 15' for the depth of the stage without the width of Browne's alley, 23' with it. The first seems an impossibly small dimension for an Elizabethan stage, but the second, though still small, is distinctly possible. The Fortune stage was 27'6" deep. If the proportion between depth and width of the stage at the Boar's Head was the same as that at the Fortune, the Boar's Head stage should have been a little more than 25' deep. The two demolished buildings, of course, could easily have been less than 15' deep, so that the stage could have been 25' deep.

Persons in the "wedges" at the sides of the stage, in the space between the front and the long building, and in the galleries all had full view of the stage. Persons in the north and south extremities of the yard did not. But even the worst positioned of these—in the northwest or southwest corners—could see the front 8'6" or so of the stage if they could see over the heads of those in front of them. For an Elizabethan play, as the Swan drawing would suggest, perhaps that was enough.

IV

If the Boar's Head ceased to be a playhouse by 1621, it had probably ceased to be an inn much earlier. Not a single stable is mentioned in the deeds of 1621, except the certain other buildings formerly called a stable. The Boar's Head may have ceased to be an inn in 1600 so that its controllers could abide by the Privy Council order of that year which forbade acting in inns. In any case, the receiving of travellers had long been only part of the function of the place. Certainly there were plenty of people who had permanent residences there in the 1590s and at least a few who did as far back as 1581.

Needler's and Browne's alleys must have been built promptly—Needler's because Browne was buying the strip of the yard which many inhabitants had to use to get out of the inn via the main entrance in Whitechapel, and Browne's because it gave access to the eight or nine structures he meant to build on the stage plot. The pulling down of buildings on the western side of the yard in 1621 no doubt had something to do with the making of both alleys.

By the time of Ogilby and Morgan, the stage plot had been built over and the great barn replaced by a welter of small holdings. The long building remained, as did the entrance into Whitechapel (reached now by many inhabitants through Browne's strip in front of the long building). The only part of the yard which remained open was the northern extremity, apparently once called the courtyard.

By the time of Rocque's map (1746), the entrance on Whitechapel was gone, and so were the passages leading immediately to it. They had probably become new buildings and gardens or yards belonging to them. All but the northernmost 25' or so of Browne's alley had also disappeared, but, as we shall see, its whole length remained a property line. The courtyard was now joined by a short passage to the next enclave north, which Ogilby and Morgan called Tripe Yard, but which Rocque and his successors also called Boar's Head Yard (the name Tripe Yard having retreated to the alley which had once led from that yard into Petticoat Lane). The northern parts of the long building remained, or at least structures built on their sites, as did Browne's access strip to some of them. Needler's alley also remained. The surviving vestiges of the stage plot were the northern line along Needler's alley and the part of the western line which Browne's alley marked.

This dispensation also appears in Horwood's map (1792-99), except that by then Browne's alley was entirely gone, though it continued as a property line. The northern and western lines of the stage plot continued as they had in Rocque's time. By now, if not in Rocque's time, most of the stage plot had lost its buildings and returned to open space.

Rocque's dispensation even appears in the map (1:500) drawn to accompany a surveyor's report of June 15, 1849, on the Metropolitan sewers in and around Goulston Street.[31] It is the most de-

[31] G.L.C., J.Ste/5871.

tailed map of the place since Ogilby and Morgan, and for the first time since the seventeenth century one need not guess what has happened to the stage plot. The three premises which Ogilby and Morgan show along the front of the stage have now joined Rowley's property. The four which they show in the northwest angle of the stage plot, those bound on the west and south by Browne's alley, are still together, and now form an open yard divided into six parts. Three rather than two are on the west side and the same on the east. The parts on the west side are still directly north of the third house on Whitechapel after Middlesex Street (since the eighteenth century 146 Whitechapel High Street) and the parts on the east are still directly north of the fourth (Browne's house, now 145 Whitechapel High Street). Nine premises still stand on Whitechapel between Middlesex Street (Hog Lane in Ogilby and Morgan) and Goulston Street (Boar's Head Alley in Ogilby and Morgan). As in Ogilby and Morgan, the eastern line of this plot is still more or less flush with the western side of the courtyard.

Except for amalgamations in the northwest angle of the stage plot (six properties become two) and on Whitechapel, this dispensation also appears in the first detailed Ordnance Survey map of the place, surveyed in 1873, published (1:1056) in 1875.

Much of this old arrangement disappeared at last between about 1875 and the Ordnance Survey map of 1894-96. The Metropolitan Board of Works acquired and then cleared the northern half of the Boar's Head site and much else still farther north and east. It built there ranges of very solid and very typical flats for "the working class," some of which, north of the Boar's Head site, still exist. It sold these in the 1880s to persons who agreed to keep them decent and use the property for nothing else for eighty years from 1884. Much of the southern half of the site became Aldgate East station on the Metropolitan Railway. Goulston Street to the east was rebuilt and widened, and so were parts of Middlesex Street. In the process, the site of the Boar's Head lost about 35' of its width. The structure on the site of the long building and Browne's access to it, the courtyard—what Ogilby and Morgan had called Tripe Yard —all disappeared. Only Needler's alley survived and, strangely, the property lines of the yard in the northwest angle of the stage plot.

Needler's alley had gone by the name Boar's Head Yard since at least 1856. It now ran about 74'3" into the Boar's Head site from the edge of buildings in Middlesex Street—its full length ordained in Needler's deed and about a third of the way across the court-yard. A drawing of the property in the northwest angle of the stage plot appears with a deed of 1885.[32] Its title was registered in 1907 as no. 125655, now in the Harrow Land Registry. Its property lines were as they had always been, Needler's alley on the north and Browne's alley on the west and south. Its dimen-sions vary somewhat, partly because its north and east sides de-pended on two alleys which could be encroached or widened and its west side on one:

	o & m	SEWER	DEED	O.S. 1873	O.S. 1894-6	O.S. 1913
NORTH SIDE	29′9″°	28′6″	28′6″	30′	28′	27′6″
SOUTH SIDE	29′9″°	27′6″	28′	30′9″	26′3″	26′3″
WEST SIDE	31′9″	32′9″	27′4″	30′	30′1″	30′3″
EAST SIDE	30′3″	34′	27′	?	28′	28′

It was this dispensation which German bombs levelled in 1940 and 1944.

After the war, the site was used for a car park for nearly twenty years, and Needler's alley remained a piece of the King's highway leading into the place. In 1964, finally, when the eighty years exacted by the Metropolitan Board of Works were up, a large building and a smaller one attached to it rose on the northern and most of the southern parts of the site. Needler's alley disappeared at last, after some 340 years, and with it the name Boar's Head. The large building contains Cromlech House and United Stan-dard House, the small one the premises of Daylin Ltd., makers of shirts. Cromlech House, which is in the north, is open on its street level, and it is here that the Petticoat Lane Market takes place on Sundays. United Standard House is in the south and lies over most of the site of the Boar's Head. When these buildings were rising, four less pretentious shops also rose, one on Goulston Street and three which cover the frontage on Whitechapel. A sub-way for pedestrians under Whitechapel was dug and a spacious entry built on the corner of Whitechapel and Middlesex Street,

[32] Harrow Land Registry, LN186342; Middlesex Land Registry, 1885/7/392-3. I am indebted to Mr. Keller, the agent for Petticoat Lane Rentals, who kindly remembered for me the place as it was.

in front of the southern part of United Standard House. This
entry lies where the premises along Hog Lane once lay, behind
the stage plot on the south and, perhaps, behind the hostry and
residence of the Poleys on the north.

If Goulston Street existed in Elizabethan times, it was the alley
behind the long building which Ogilby and Morgan called Boar's
Head Alley. It was not part of the inn. Its southern parts were rebuilt between 1678 and 1688 by Sir William Goulston, an insur-
ance underwriter and merchant, out of property he had inherited
from an uncle, William Meggs, and bought from others. Goulston
probably also used the alley to the east, Hartshorne Alley.[33]

The site has grown considerably narrower by the widening of
Goulston Street, and frequent widenings and realignments of
Middlesex Street and its sidewalks. It is, however, the aura of the
last half of this century cast by Cromlech House and its adjuncts
which renders the Elizabethan scale of things absurd. Looking at
the site now, one cannot really bring oneself to believe that it
once contained, among other things, numerous dwellings, open
places, a great barn, and a large stage with galleries on all four
sides. That a man's castle could be 12'6" square or even less is
scarcely credible in the shadow of Cromlech House, but there
were thousands of such places in Ogilby and Morgan and no
doubt in the London of seventy-five years before.

Finally the blue plaque. Despite all the building and rebuilding
in the Boar's Head these four hundred years, especially that in
Victorian and our own times, three things remain. Almost in-
credibly they are the west, south, and east lines of the property
in the northwest angle of the stage plot, for the southern extremity of United Standard House occupies the whole of the land
represented in title 125655 and no more.[34] That extremity houses
the Carpet Supermarket of the Mercantile Carpet Co. The
southern thirty feet or so of its store front on Middlesex Street,
therefore, lies along Browne's alley "right descending" from

[33] P.C.C. 41 Reeve and 4 Exton; C.P.25(2)/692/Hil. 33&34 Chas. II/16; and a
series of lawsuits which began on Sir William's death in 1688 and continued until
the 1730s. In these and in numerous mortgages which his son, Morris, put on the
property, no one mentioned the Boar's Head: C.7/572/46; C.9/447/153, 154;
C.8/452/41; /467/63, 74; C.9/460/1; /469/69; C.11/1463/20; C.24/1247; /1252;
Middlesex Land Registry, 1724/2/249; 1726/1/107; 1730/4/400; 1731/2/119;
1734/3/437, etc.
[34] Cromlech House and its adjuncts occupy land registered as titles no. 125655,
349523, LN43535, LN52027, LN95656, LN186342, and LN103162. With one excep-

Needler's alley, and most of the western edge of the stage plot. The next eight or nine feet south, along the front of a clothing store, are the rest of that edge. The Greater London Council may put their blue plaque anywhere on those store fronts along this distance. The northern limit, and therefore the northwest corner of the stage plot, is national grid reference TQ 33830/81306.

APPENDIX: The Accuracy of Ogilby and Morgan's Map

It is impossible to say exactly how well Ogilby and Morgan measured the Boar's Head, and it is treacherous to try to establish how well they may have done it. Not a single building in the vicinity survived unaltered until the first detailed Ordnance Survey maps, 1848-50 and 1873-75, nor, probably, did a single thoroughfare survive unencroached upon, or unwidened, or unbuilt over. A few property lines may have survived, in the great yard of the Boar's Head and in and around Gun Square, but all have been subject to three centuries of encroachment and bad surveying. Moreover, one cannot depend for fine measurements on maps in general, much less on one three hundred years old. Draughtsmen and engravers cannot draw lines with complete accuracy, nor can we measure them so, and even if they and we could, maps do not lie still. The Ordnance Survey calculates that its large-scale maps may be accurate only down to three feet.[35]

Ogilby and Morgan's scale bar, unluckily, suggests but does not resolve the problems caused by shrinkage and expansion of paper. The bar and the Boar's Head are on different sheets. The printing of the sheets of the map was no doubt like that of the sheets of books, one going through the press for its full run and then another. The printing of the Boar's Head sheet in any com-

tion these represent the yard of 1849 and everything north of it between Middlesex and Goulston Streets to well beyond the Boar's Head site. The exception is LN-80561, which G.L.C. acquired, consisting of a piece still vacant on Goulston Street, a strip along Middlesex Street, and a piece on the north corner of Needler's alley and Middlesex Street. G.L.C. used the strip to realign Middlesex Street yet again and the piece north of Needler's alley to have room for the entrance to the subway for pedestrians under Whitechapel. I am indebted to the mortgage holders, Sun Life of Canada, and to the owners of Cromlech House, City and Country Properties, Ltd., for help in identifying the titles and permission to see the abstracts of them.
[35] D. A. Hutchinson, "Co-ordination of Mining Surveys with the Ordnance Survey," *Transactions of the Institution of Mining Engineers*, LXXVI (1928-29), 299-312.

plete map, therefore, necessarily has no connection with that of the scale bar sheet. A look at the map under glass on the wall at Guildhall demonstrates the problem. All its sheets are mounted side by side so that the whole map is spread before one. Some of its sheets are heavily inked, some lightly, and some match one or more of their neighbours well, others less well. Besides, most surviving copies of the map are probably pasted on to cloth or heavy paper to preserve them. Distortion must occur in the thorough wetting involved here, and in binding the sheets to a material which must shrink and expand at different rates from the original paper. Needless to say, much will also depend on where and how the map has been kept for three hundred years.

I have seen five copies of the map: the Crace copy and the other at the British Museum (MAPS C.7.b.4), the wall copy and the strongroom copy at Guildhall, and the copy at G.L.C. The Boar's Head sheets are all different from one another by as much as 1/8" measured diagonally for a foot across the centre, and the scale bar sheets by more than 1/16" in the five inches of the bar. It even seems that one copy of a sheet may be smaller than its fellows in one part and larger in another. One map (like the strong-room one) may have a big Boar's Head sheet and a small scale bar one. I calculate these differences, however, at no more than ± 1/64" in an inch, or, on Ogilby and Morgan's scale, 1'7" in 100'.

The best of these five maps is that at G.L.C. Sheet for sheet, it is the best preserved, and it also seems the most consistent in printing. It alone is not pasted fully onto backing; each sheet is pasted only along the top on to the leaves of a large book. The Boar's Head sheet, measured diagonally across its centre, is in the middle of the range of the same sheet in the other maps (though its scale bar sheet is one of the small ones). I have assumed that this copy fairly represents the middle size of those surviving and calculated the middle size of the scale bar at about 2 per cent less than the five inches it shows. I have used this copy, therefore, for all my measurements, and I have added 2 per cent to them. I hope thereby to have arrived at something like what was on Ogilby and Morgan's plates.

Arrived at in this way, Ogilby and Morgan's dimensions between streets and alleys which survived until 1848-50 and 1873, and around properties which seem to have kept their shapes, are impressively reliable.

The main thoroughfares around the Boar's Head survived until the Ordnance Survey maps (they survive still) and so did a few minor ones, though all altered in many ways. Even so, Ogilby and Morgan's dimensions between these thoroughfares are very close to those of the Ordnance Survey maps, except around corners much developed, like that of Houndsditch and Whitechapel, and The Minories and Whitechapel, and around entrances to alleys and yards which seem to have moved. There Ogilby and Morgan's margin of error (if that is what it is, and if the Ordnance Survey maps may be taken as accurate) is as high as 19.3 per cent, but over longer distances in which such changes were subsumed, their error is slight indeed, 2.5 per cent or less. The surviving streets on the north side of Whitechapel in the sheet which contains the Boar's Head begin along Houndsditch with Gravel Lane, then Gun Square (Yard in 1676), Church Row, and Whitechapel itself; along Whitechapel, Three Nuns Yard, Bull Inn, and Black Horse Yard (White Horse Yard in 1676); and along Middlesex Street (Hog Lane in Elizabethan and Jacobean times, then Petticoat Lane for 150 years), and Needler's alley. The distances between them are:

	O & M	O.S.	Amount by which O & M differ
Gravel Lane to Gun Square	56'3"	55'	+ 2.27%
Gun Square to Church Row	114'9"	117'	– 1.92%
Church Row to Whitechapel	253'	253'	0%
Houndsditch to Three Nuns Yd.	162'7"	182'	–10.66%
Three Nuns Yd. to Bull Inn	186'5"	182'2"	+ 2.33%
Bull Inn to Black Horse Yd.	133'6"	135'3"	– 1.29%
Black Horse Yd. to Mddx. St.	103'10"	87'	+19.34%
Whitechapel to Needler's alley	162'7"	159'6"	+ 1.92%
	1,172'11"	1,170'11"	+ 0.17%

On the south side of Whitechapel four streets survived: The Minories, Harrow Alley (now Little Somerset St.), Irish Court, and Halfmoon Passage. The distances between them are as follow:

The Minories to Harrow Alley	287'8"	302'6"	− 4.96%
Harrow Alley to Irish Court	331'6"	311'	+ 6.59%
Irish Court to Halfmoon Passage	231'	217'3"	+ 5.98%
	851'2"	830'9"	+ 2.45%

The entrances to the alleys on the north side of Whitechapel and to Harrow Alley may have moved with repeated rebuilding.

Gun Square is probably worth looking at because alone among the yards, courts, and alleys in the vicinity of the Boar's Head it more or less kept its shape until the Second World War, especially about its entrance. Even here, however, all the buildings were rebuilt at least once, the entrance and yard probably encroached upon, and Houndsditch outside widened. Still, around those properties which seem to have kept their shapes, Ogilby and Morgan are off no more than 8.7 per cent between points which would have been obvious to their chainmen and 10.8 per cent between those which would not have been obvious.

The four premises on the north side of the entrance in 1873 stood where five had stood in 1676, but seem to have kept the lines of the five. The four premises on the south side of the entrance in 1873 were also five in Ogilby and Morgan and they, too, seem to have kept the lines of their predecessors. The property in the southwest corner of the yard stayed within its lines, too. The dimensions are:

	O & M	O.S.	Amount by which O & M differ
Entrance, north side	76'	74'	+ 2.70%
south side	44'8"	47'	− 4.96%
Width of the square after the entrance	41'10"	38'6"	+ 8.65%

Four new buildings on
  the north side of the
  entrance

east line	29′*	32′6″	−10.76%
west line	28′5″*	29′	− 2.01%
north line	42′6″*	42′	+ 1.19%
south line	43′6″	44′	− 1.13%

Four new buildings on the
  south side of the entrance

north line	44′8″	47′	− 4.96%
south line	47′6″*	47′	+ 1.06%
east & west lines	31′3″*	32′	− 2.34%

Property in the southwest
  corner of the yard
  north & south

lines	18′*	18′	0%
east line	27′*	27′	0%
west line	26′6″*	26′6″	0%

Could we hold Ogilby and Morgan against the geography of their own time, therefore, we should probably find their chainmen generally accurate to ± 3 to 4 per cent, and frequently better, rarely off more than 8 per cent and then for dimensions which they would have had trouble measuring. Their men, however, were better with chains than with theodolites, for the main streets leave Whitechapel at somewhat inaccurate angles. Still, for their time, and for our purpose, Ogilby and Morgan were right to call their work "This Most Accurate Survey."

No one, incidentally, seems to have noticed that Ogilby and Morgan have an outline of the Duke's Theatre, apparently carefully drawn, from which we might supply an important hiatus in our knowledge of that house. They show the theatre, slightly out of square, as about 57′4″ east and west, about 138′ north and south. As in other evidence, on the south end is a portico (not included in the 138′) held up by four columns. The portico is about 15′ deep and runs the full width of the building. Measured from their centres, the columns are about 17′ apart, about 12′6″ from the wall behind them, and about 5′ in diameter. These dimensions are probably reliable, especially because the building is isolated from streets and other buildings.

The Ordnance Survey first surveyed Whitechapel for a large-scale map in 1848-50. The resulting map, however, is a "skeleton" one, showing only streets. The Ordnance Survey filled in this map in a survey of 1873, for the new map published in 1875. The Ordnance Survey revised it in 1894-6, and (for Land Registry purposes) in 1913; the L.C.C. revised it in 1938. All these maps are to the scale 1:1056. The Ordnance Survey re-surveyed Whitechapel in the late 1960s and issued a new map to the scale 1:1250 in 1969. For the measurements in which I compare the Ordnance Survey and Ogilby and Morgan, I use the map of 1873-75, the copy at the British Museum (it differs only rarely from that of 1848-50). I refer to the other maps as appropriate, and use that of 1969 in my remarks about the present state of the site. I have measured in a straight line across property fronts from the middle of one street to the middle of the next. I should have halved, therefore, differences caused by alterations to one side of a corner and avoided or reduced those caused by alterations to both sides.

Shakespeare and
the Second Blackfriars

J. A. LAVIN

In reviewing the revised edition of Frederic E. Faverty's *The Victorian Poets*, in the Spring (1970) issue of *Victorian Poetry*, Kenneth Allott remarks:

> An indirect consequence of the plethora of material that now bids for our attention is the lowering of the whole standard of intellectual debate by the "live-and-let-live" policy we have tacitly adopted to critical extravagance. It is a subjective impression, but I believe that our sense of what constitutes evidence in critical discussion has been eroded in recent years, and that we are often reluctant to determine whether or not an idea has been expressed distinctly or an argument been made to tell. Life is too short, we say apologetically, to be spent in repelling modish imbecilities, but the consequence is that the imbecilities are left uncontroverted. (88)

He continues:

> The point I am making is that our culpable toleration of critical extravagance and irresponsibility in method, content, and expression springs at least partly from our inability when so much is being published to nail one absurdity before the next comes along. (89)

Carelessness is endemic in every area of literary scholarship, and is found as often in Shakespearean studies as in those devoted to Victorian or modern writers. It is difficult to decide whether it is more damaging when discovered lurking behind the conclusions of critical explication or theatrical history, or encountered as bald statement in handbooks for students. One such volume, published in 1967, remarks that "Shakespeare's stage had, of course, no artificial lighting and only an occasional suggestion of locale or setting. This limitation worked to his advantage and ours, for many of the most memorable passages in his plays result from his setting a scene for us in words—a task which we today leave to the lighting technician and scene designer."[1] The difficulty with this assertion derives from the thoughtless use of the phrase "Shakespeare's stage." Whether it is employed as a synonym for that other commonly misused generic label "the Elizabethan stage," or whether it is intended to allude to a single particular stage on which Shakespeare's plays were performed, the phrase necessarily negates the truth of the proposition it introduces, for while it is true that the Globe stage did not make use of artificial lighting (I am discounting hand-props such as candles, lanterns, and torches), the plays were also performed on other stages which did. Quite apart from those of Shakespeare's plays which were performed at the Second Blackfriars after it became available in 1609, *The Comedy of Errors* was presented at Gray's Inn in 1594, *Twelfth Night* at the Middle Temple in 1602, *Macbeth* at Hampton Court in 1606, *Pericles* at Whitehall in 1619, and several of his other plays at court on various dates. Moreover, some of the Chamberlain's and King's Men's plays which had originally been produced at the Globe were revived indoors at the Blackfriars, and vice versa. The notion that the physical characteristics of a particular theatre determined or heavily affected the literary features of plays is one to which I shall return, for it has gone virtually unquestioned, and lies behind many such statements as that just noticed; but before I do so, one variant of scholarly method deriving from the same assumption may be mentioned.

While on the one hand it is believed that a knowledge of a theatre's structure can be drawn upon to explain certain features of a play's literary text, an obverse method has been employed to identify the theatre for which a play was allegedly first written, by examining allusions in the text. Thus, the handbook already mentioned says, presumably on the evidence of the Prologue's reference to "this wooden O," that Shakespeare's *Henry V* "opened the Globe Theatre, built from the salvaged timbers of the old playhouse, The Theatre" (p. 86). Unfortunately, "this wooden

---

[1] David and Mita Scott Hedges, *Speaking Shakespeare* (New York, 1967), p. 28.

O" refers, almost certainly, not the the Globe, but to the Curtain, because the Essex references in the Chorus to Act V can hardly have been written later than June 1599, while the Globe was not completed until August or September of that year.[2] So any literary-critical conclusions about the influence of the physical arrangements of the Globe theatre or its stage on Shakespeare's style in *Henry V*, or on the structure or dramaturgy of that play, are wrong.

More important than whether *Henry V* was first performed at the Curtain or at the Globe is the assumption that prompts the concern and the argument about the play's place of first performance. It has become established as an article of faith in theatrical history that the physical arrangements of the Elizabethan and Jacobean playhouses largely determined the dramaturgy of the playwrights, and that they wrote not only with one company and even the individual actors of that company in mind, but also with a view to the facilities and limitations of a particular playhouse.[3] Moreover, differences in the composition of the audiences at the public and private theatres have been adduced as evidence to show that playwrights also consciously catered to the different tastes of audiences at the different theatres, as well as to the different tastes of groundlings and the gallery within a single audience. Such a thesis is central in Alfred Harbage's *Shakespeare's Audience* (New York, 1941), and in his *Shakespeare and the Rival Traditions* (New York, 1952).

In particular, by a combination of these various assumptions it has been asserted that the acquisition of the Blackfriars Theatre by the King's Men in 1609 brought about a complete change in Shakespeare's methods and style, and that the last plays show him, like Beaumont and Fletcher, writing plays to suit a courtly audience whose theatrical tastes had been affected by the court masque, and who would appreciate the finer dramatic effects now possible in the indoor theatre by the use of artificial light.[4]

This argument has been most fully expounded by G. E. Bentley in his essay "Shakespeare and the Blackfriars Theatre" (*Shake-*

[2] Cf. E. K. Chambers, *The Elizabethan Stage* (Oxford, 1923), II, 402.

[3] See, for example, *T. W. Baldwin, The Organization and Personnel of the Shakespearean Company* (Princeton, 1927).

[4] See J. Isaacs, *Production and Stage Management at the Blackfriars Theatre* (London, 1933), p. 5; H. Granville-Barker, *Prefaces to Shakespeare* (Princeton, 1946), I, 470-471; G. E. Bentley, *Shakespeare and His Theatre* (Lincoln, Nebraska, 1964), pp. 78-79.

peare Survey 1, 1948), reprinted in modified form in his *Shake-
speare and his Theatre* (1964), and in Clifford Leech's edition of
The Two Noble Kinsmen, (The New Signet Shakespeare, 1966).
Bentley's conclusions have been widely accepted, for instance by
Bernard Beckerman who, in *Shakespeare at the Globe* (New
York, 1962), says:

> In 1608-1609 the King's Men, acquiring the private indoor theatre of
> Blackfriars, brought the distinctive [Globe] period to a close, for with
> the leasing of Blackfriars, according to Professor Gerald Bentley,
> came a change of outlook.... Altogether the events grouped around
> the move to Blackfriars indicate that then too a new start was made,
> and Bentley convincingly demonstrates that within a short time
> Blackfriars became the leading playhouse for the King's Men in point
> of prestige and profit. (p. xi.)

Clifford Leech, in his article, "The Dramatists' Independence"
(*Research Opportunities in Renaissance Drama,* X, 1967), comments:

> Professor Bentley in *Shakespeare and His Theatre* has considered
> several key-moments in Shakespeare's career where the influence of
> members of his company was likely to be particularly strong. Nothing
> that I have to say here contradicts that. (18)

Lastly, and most recently, Professor Schoenbaum has this year
remarked that Professor Bentley's essay is "surely one of the most
important articles on Shakespeare to be published in the past
quarter century," and says in summary,

> Although we have little certain information regarding the theatrical
> provenance of Shakespeare's last plays, it is not unreasonable to sup-
> pose that —except for *Henry VIII*—he wrote with an eye to the special
> conditions at the Blackfriars. This factor may help to account for the
> new direction taken by his art in *Cymbeline, The Winter's Tale,* and
> *The Tempest.*[5]

Professor Bentley's arguments, then, merit examination. He
begins by listing six events which seem to have been important in
the affairs of the Chamberlain's–King's company, and which "one
would expect to have influenced his [Shakespeare's] work" (p.

[5] S. Schoenbaum, "Shakespeare the Ignoramus," *The Drama of the Renaissance:
Essays for Leicester Bradner,* ed. Elmer M. Blistein (Providence, 1970), p. 162.

66). [6] These events are: the closing of the theatres by the plague in 1593 and 1594; the resulting formation of the company; the building of the first Globe; the Essex rebellion; the attaining of the King's patronage on the death of Elizabeth; and the acquisition of the Blackfriars.

This initial concern to emphasize that we should regard Shakespeare as "above all else a man of the theatre" (p. 71) rather than as "the poet, preparing his plays with constant consideration for the reader in the study" (p. 65), is perfectly proper, even if, in these days, somewhat unnecessary, and there is little point in cavilling at the choice of significant events. It should be mentioned, however, that acceptance of the major premise which categorizes Shakespeare as "above all else a man of the theatre" tends to create a false dichotomy between Shakespeare the man of the theatre and Shakespeare the creative artist, a danger recognized by Professor Schoenbaum in his article on "Shakespeare the Ignoramus" when he warns us against "that most ghastly *reductio ad absurdum* of all, according to which *King Lear* is show biz" (p. 163).

If one recognizes that Shakespeare was a businessman, a professional dramatist, and a poet, it becomes necessary to make some distinctions, for while events which "seem to have been important" in the affairs of the Chamberlain's–King's company may well have been so, and while such events may also have been important to Shakespeare the businessman, they may have had little or no importance for Shakespeare the artist. One of the most significant events in Virginia Woolf's professional career was the establishment of the Hogarth Press, but one would hardly attribute to it the difference in method and style that is discernible between *The Voyage Out*, published by Duckworth in 1916, and *Jacob's Room*, published by the Hogarth Press six years later. It may be asked whether, in his insistence on seeing Shakespeare solely as a professional theatre man, Bentley has not thrown out the baby with Edmund Dowden's biographical bathwater, and whether such exclusiveness is finally any less fallacious than treating the plays as documents of Shakespeare's spiritual biography. When Bentley chooses six particular events and asserts that "one would expect" them "to have influenced" Shakespeare's work, is the position he has adopted really any more respectable aca-

[6] Subsequent page references are to the modified version of Bentley's essay in *Shakespeare and His Theatre*.

70

demically than that held by someone who claims that "one would expect the death of Shakespeare's heir and only son Hamnet at the age of eleven in 1596 to have influenced his work"?

My use of the rhetorical question is deliberate, for it and the word "surely" figure largely in Bentley's argumentative method. Thus, in referring to the building of the first Globe in 1599, he says:

> Here was a theatre built for the occupancy of a particular company, and six of the seven owners were actors in the company. Assuredly it was built, so far as available funds would allow, to the specific requirements of the productions of the Lord Chamberlain's Men. What facilities did Shakespeare get which he had not had before? How did he alter his composition to take advantage of the new possibilities? Can there be any doubt that as a successful man of the theatre he did so? (p. 67)

The inherent weakness of the rhetorical question is that it may not receive the affirmative or negative answer which it intends. The first Globe was constructed of the dismantled timbers of the Theatre, and as the timbers would presumably have been re-assembled in their original relationships so as to take advantage of the original cutting and jointing,[7] we may suppose that the first Globe, built in 1599, was of the same size as the Theatre, built about twenty-five years earlier, in 1576,[8] and essentially identical in its main features. The first Globe was, in fact, the old Theatre built by James Burbage in Shoreditch, and now re-erected on the Bankside, renamed and refurbished, but it had been occupied successively by Leicester's, Warwick's–Oxford's, the Queen's, and the Admiral's for twenty years before the Chamberlain's Men settled there from 1594-96. The certitude of Bentley's statement, "assuredly it was built . . . to the specific requirements of the productions of the Lord Chamberlain's men," is therefore not warranted by the facts.

Moreover, his question, "what facilities did Shakespeare get which he had not had before?" must consequently receive the answer, "probably none of any significance." Similarly, "how did he alter his composition to take advantage of the new possibilities?" (which Bentley does not specify), must be answered, "we don't know, and he probably didn't." Lastly, to "can there be

---

[7] Irwin Smith, "Theatre into Globe," *SQ*, III (1952), 113-120.
[8] Richard Hosley, "Elizabethan Theatres and Audiences," *RORD*, X (1967), 11.

any doubt that as a successful man of the theatre he did so?" I reply yes.

Furthermore, I assert categorically that there is not a shred of evidence to show that the dramaturgy of Elizabethan playwrights was materially affected by the physical arrangements of the public playhouses, and that in fact all the available evidence points in the opposite direction, as I argued here last year.[9] There is no time to rehearse those arguments, which were based largely on the facts of theatrical history recorded in Henslowe's *Diary*, but it may be reasserted that versatility and not specialization was required of the individual actor, because of the practice of doubling roles within a single play, and because of the huge number of parts he played in any one season. The actor's versatility even made it possible for one character to be played by different actors within the same performance. C. J. Sisson, in his edition of the Massinger holograph of *Believe as you List,* a King's Men play licensed in 1631, remarks:

> It is interesting to observe that the characters Calistus and Demetrius are presented in Act I by Baxter and Pattrick, and in Act II by Hobbes and Balls, a third actor, "Rowland," taking over the part of Demetrius in Act III.[10]

Henslowe's *Diary* demonstrates that the complexity, variety and flexibility of Elizabethan dramatic activity demanded virtuosity and adaptability, not only from the individual actor but also from the whole troupe, for companies such as the Admiral's Men acted under conditions which varied greatly. They performed in the provinces and at court as well as in London, and in inn-yards, town halls, royal palaces, college halls, private dwellings, the Inns of Court, and various permanent playhouses ranging from the Theatre in 1576 to the Fortune in the 1620s. It was common for individual actors to move to and from the Admiral's Men and other companies, which merged with, and absorbed each other, as well as playing jointly, sharing each other's repertories, and buying each other's plays. Henslowe's *Diary* and other evidence clearly demonstrates the capacity of the different companies for dealing with almost any play that was put into their hands, and their ability to act such plays in virtually any surroundings.

[9] J. A. Lavin, "The Inductive Method and the Elizabethan Theatre," *The Elizabethan Theatre II*, ed. David Galloway (Toronto, 1970).
[10] *Malone Society Reprints* (Oxford, 1927), p. xxii.

If a particular play was originally written for one company and one theatre, that fact quickly lost whatever relevance it may once have had. Of Shakespeare's early plays, *I Henry VI* was probably first performed in 1592 by Lord Strange's Men at the Rose. The *True Tragedy (III Henry VI)* was introduced before 1595 by the Earl of Pembroke's Servants at a playhouse not specified; *Richard III*, presumably the play that Henslowe refers to as "Buckingham" in his diary, was played by Sussex's Men in 1593, probably at the Rose. *Titus Andronicus* was produced by at least four companies before 1594: those of the Earl of Derby, the Earl of Pembroke, the Earl of Sussex, and (at Newington Butts) either the Lord Chamberlain's Men or the Lord Admiral's, or the two companies jointly. It was also possible, for instance, to revive Marlowe's *Edward II* at the Red Bull in 1620, and *Friar Bacon* at the Fortune in 1630. More importantly for present purposes, the central argument which Alfred Harbage attempts to establish in *Shakespeare and the Rival Traditions*, that there were "two distinct theatrical traditions in England, signalized by two distinct kinds of theatre," the public and private, which, he claims, had different repertories, mainly satiric comedy at the private theatres, but "romantic, idealistic, positive, and often patriotic and religious" plays at the public theatres, is not substantiated by the facts. As one would expect, the companies did not make this kind of distinction in their repertories, for private theatre plays were performed at the public theatres and vice versa, and, even more damaging to Harbage's argument, both public and private theatre plays were performed for the sophisticated and socially exclusive audience at court. Not enough attention has been paid to this interchangeability of repertories, although Richard Hosley has pointed out that

> *Satiromastix* (presumably a public theatre play) was performed by different companies at the Globe and the theatre of the Paul's Boys; *The Malcontent* (evidently a private theatre play) by different companies at the Blackfriars and the Globe; and several plays, such as *Philaster*, by the same company at the Blackfriars and the Globe.[11]

It may also be remembered that, according to the title-page of the 1623 quarto, *The Duchess of Malfi* was "Presented privately,

[11] "Elizabethan Theatres and Audiences," p. 14.

at the Blackfriars, and publicly at the Globe," and that the 1629 quarto of *Lovers Melancholy* describes it as "Acted at the Private House in the Black Friars, and publicly at the Globe."

From these assorted facts the following conclusions may be derived: first, that the Theatre, metamorphosed into the first Globe, was unlikely to offer Shakespeare any new possibilities of a dramaturgic sort; second, that in any case the physical arrangements of the public theatres were not of prime concern to either the actors or the playwrights; third, that Shakespeare did not, therefore, "alter his composition" as a consequence of the building of the Globe. If he did, the results are not discernible. I challenge anyone to identify for me those characteristics of the Globe plays, from *Much Ado* to *Pericles*, which distinguish them from the pre-Globe plays, *Comedy of Errors* to *Henry V*, and which are explicable in terms of arrangements at the Globe.

Given the interchangeability of public, private, and court theatre repertories, it seems to me equally unlikely that a major shift in Shakespeare's methods was necessitated, or even prompted by, the acquisition of the Blackfriars in 1609, to which I now turn.

I alluded earlier to Bentley's fondness for the rhetorical question, and to his propensity for attaching to speculative statements the words "surely," "assuredly," and "must." In noting the increased frequency of court performances (about thirteen a year) by the King's Men after their attainment of James I's patronage, he says:

> a good part of their time must have been devoted to the preparation of command performances. Surely this new status of the troupe must have been a steady and pervasive influence in the development of its principal dramatist, William Shakespeare. (p. 69)

But for years Whitehall had used what would now be called a legal fiction in justifying London performances to the city authorities; namely, that they were all rehearsals for performance at court,[12] and one must not therefore attach too much theatrical significance to the company's change of name and patron and its so-called new status. Not only does the ratio of the number of court performances to public performances put

[12] Chambers, *Elizabethan Stage*, IV, 312.

into perspective the relative importance of the former in terms of the King's Men's total activity, but the records show that from an economic point of view the return on court performances was a small fraction of the company's total income.

Using Baldwin's figures and Henslowe's *Diary*, an average of two hundred playing days a year in London between 1594 and 1596 produced a return of £840. Harbage estimated the average yearly income at the Rose during the same period at £1,400; and a combination of Harbage's attendance figures and J. C. Adams' arrangement of the Globe yields an annual average of £1,724. Between 1599 and 1609 the average annual total for playing at court received by the Chamberlain's-King's Men "was 77 pounds 6 shillings, with the court payments in the later years substantially greater than in the early ones. Grants from Elizabeth never totalled more than 5 per cent of the income the company earned at the Globe. Under James the percentage rose to a high of about fifteen by 1609."[13]

The evidence contradicts Bentley's assertion that after 1603 "a good part of their time must have been devoted to the preparation of command performances." Very few plays received their first performances by professional troupes at court, and Bernard Beckerman has shown that, "of 144 plays presented at Court between 1590 and 1642, only eight seem to have been intended especially and initially for the Court. Two were presented in 1620, five after 1629. Only one comes from the first decade of the seventeenth century." And, it may be added, there is some doubt about that one (*As Merry As May Be*).[14]

What Queen Elizabeth and King James saw performed at court by Shakespeare and his fellows were plays chosen from the Chamberlain's-King's Men repertory which had been proven in their London playhouses before the general public. These facts seriously undermine Bentley's assurance about the effects produced by the Chamberlain's Men becoming the King's Men: "surely this new status of the troupe must have been a steady and pervasive influence in the development of its principal dramatist William Shakespeare." It may even be argued that the change of name did not really constitute a change in status, for Queen Elizabeth had patronized the company as

[13] Bernard Beckerman, *Shakespeare at the Globe* (New York, 1962), p. 22; Chambers, *Elizabethan Stage*, IV, 166-175.
[14] Beckerman, p. 20.

James continued to do, and the real purpose that lay behind the Lord Chamberlain's handing over of his company at the Globe to King James—the Earl of Nottingham's surrendering his company and interest in the Fortune to Prince Henry, and the passing of Worcester's company to Queen Anne was, as has been shown by Glynne Wickham, the extension of the Privy Council's control of the theatres, and the prevention of further multiplication of companies and playhouses.[15] On July 7, 1604, the Elizabethan statute governing "common Players of Enterludes" was revised and a nobleman's right to maintain a company of players was withdrawn.

For Bentley, however, the most important event in the affairs of the King's Men was the acquisition of the Blackfriars, because, as he says, "I do not see how it can have failed to be an influence in Shakespeare's development as a dramatist" (p. 69). That he expressed equal certainty about previous matters, which, when scrutinized, proved not to warrant certitude, should serve as a warning.

His comments on the significance of the Blackfriars acquisition, as on the other five events, are necessarily devalued because they are based on an assumption which is, in fact, a logical fallacy. Each of these events, he says, "except possibly the Essex rebellion, must have had a marked effect on the activities of Shakespeare's company and therefore on the dramatic creations of Shakespeare himself" (pp. 71-72). But even if we accept the unsupported assertion of the "must" clause, the conclusion inferred is unsound. Events which had a marked effect on the activities of the King's Men need not have had any effect on Shakespeare's dramatic creations.

Circumstantial evidence is notoriously dangerous, leading to conjecture and speculation which a single fact may contradict, but Bentley uses the style of the last plays as circumstantial evidence to prove that Shakespeare deliberately changed his methods to suit the Blackfriars. "The evidence," he says, "is to be seen in *Cymbeline, The Winter's Tale, The Tempest,* and *The Two Noble Kinsmen*" (p. 93).

Few competent critics who have read carefully through the Shakespeare canon have failed to recognize that there is something

[15] Glynne Wickham, "The Privy Council Order of 1597," *The Elizabethan Theatre* [I], ed. David Galloway (Toronto, 1969); p. 39.

different about *Cymbeline, The Winter's Tale, The Tempest*, and *The Two Noble Kinsmen*. (p. 94)

It may be noticed that *Pericles*, which most competent critics would include in the same group, has been excluded, for the very good reason that, although it demonstrates the characterstics of the last romances, we happen to know that it was a Globe play. (It was entered in the Stationers' Register in May 1608, and published in 1609.) The rejection of evidence prejudicial to one's thesis is human, but unscholarly. A more serious flaw in Bentley's method, however, is his technique of transmuting into fact a conjecture originally predicated on his larger hypothesis.

Alleging that the audience at the private theatre differed markedly from that at the public playhouse, the former being sophisticated and exclusive whereas the latter was rude and representative, and that the relatively intimate and artificially lit indoor theatre required an alteration in style of acting and therefore of composition, Bentley posits a series of meetings by the King's Men at which these new requirements were discussed. His clairvoyance also allows him to provide us with the minutes of these meetings: Beaumont and Fletcher and Jonson were hired as playwrights, and Shakespeare was persuaded to change his style to suit the Blackfriars.

Bentley's hypothesis is based on an acceptance of the major dichotomy between public and private theatres, postulated by Harbage in *Shakespeare and the Rival Traditions*, but I have argued that the general flexibility of the companies and the interchangeability of repertories shows that dichotomy to be false. Because the Chamberlain's–King's Men and other companies did not order plays specially written for court performances, there is no reason to suppose, as Bentley does, that the different audience and circumstances of the Blackfriars (even if they were as different from those in the public theatres as Harbage claims) would prompt them to order "plays prepared especially for that theatre" (p. 73). In the case of at least one, and probably two, of the four plays by Shakespeare allegedly prepared especially for the Blackfriars, the earliest recorded performance was actually at the Globe, where on April 20, 1611, Dr. Simon Forman saw *Macbeth*, and on May 15, *The Winter's Tale*. He does not record where and when he saw *Cymbeline*, but it was probably in the same theatre at about the same time. It could not have been later than September 8, 1611, on which date Forman died.

The conjecture that such meetings were held, such topics discussed, and such decisions arrived at, is introduced into Bentley's argument as a speculation, albeit with his usual certitude, but is then referred to retrospectively as an established fact. A dozen quotations will illustrate how, through the cumulative effect of repetition, conjecture is established as fact. They are given in the order of their occurrence:

(1) We can be perfectly sure, then, that from the day of the first proposal that the King's Men take over the Blackfriars they had talked among themselves about what they would do with it and had discussed what kinds of plays they would have to have written to exploit it. (pp. 75-6)

(2) We can be sure that active planning for performances at the Blackfriars did get under way when Burbage...knew for certain that the boy actors would give up their lease. (p. 77)

(3) March to July 1608, then, are the months for discussions among the King's Men of prospective performances at the Blackfriars. (p. 78)

(4) There must also have been extended discussions of what to do about the repertory. (p. 79)

(5) It seems likely that one of the foundations of their later unquestioned dominance...was their decision about plays and playwrights made in their discussions of March to July 1608. (p. 80)

(6) Possibly just before the time of the conferences of the King's Men he [Jonson] had been writing for the Blackfriars. (p. 82)

(7) Another decision, which I suggest the King's Men made at these conferences...(p. 84)

(8) This new state of affairs was just developing when the King's Men had their conferences about the Blackfriars in 1608. (p. 85)

(9) Another of the policies agreed upon at the conferences of 1608 was to secure the services of Beaumont and Fletcher. (p. 88)

(10) The third of these three important changes in policy which I think the King's Men agreed upon at their conferences about the new Blackfriars enterprise,...(p. 88)

(11) I am suggesting that in the conferences of 1608 the King's Men... persuaded William Shakespeare to devote his attention to that theatre [the Blackfriars] in the future instead of to the Globe. (p. 93)

Finally, and most astonishingly, "both [*Cymbeline* and *Phil-aster*] were written, or at least completed, after the important decision made by the leaders of the troupe in the spring of 1608 to commission new plays for Blackfriars, and both were prepared to be acted in the private theatre in Blackfriars before the sophisticated audience attracted to that house" (pp. 96-97).

Thus theory and speculation are gradually transmuted into historical fact, for which, I hope it is unnecessary to insist, there is not a single scrap of positive and direct proof.

Having dismissed the hypothetical strategy meetings of the King's Men in 1608, and with them the equally hypothetical decisions there taken, it might seem necessary to offer some alternative explanation for the peculiar character of Shakespeare's last plays. The first thing to be said is that although they are regarded by modern critics as virtually an autonomous group, they were not so regarded by Shakespeare's fellows, for when they compiled the First Folio of 1623, they showed no concern to present these plays as a related cluster, but instead, dispersed them widely through the volume. *The Tempest* is the first play in the Folio, beginning the section of comedies; *The Winter's Tale* is the last of the comedies; *Cymbeline* is the last among the tragedies, and the final play of the Folio; and *Pericles* was not included at all, but was added to the Third Folio of 1664.

These facts suggest that his colleagues in the King's Men did not regard the romances as a group generically different from the rest of the corpus, and to be set apart as Blackfriars plays. How then should they be regarded, and how is their nature to be explained, if not in terms of new playing conditions originating in a new theatre with new physical arrangements and a new audience with sophisticated theatrical tastes? The most likely answer that occurs to me does not, perhaps unfortunately, depend on anything as tangible as the acquisition of a new theatre by the King's Men, but on the other hand we seek no such occurrence to explain the violent shifts in style, materials, and genres in other parts of the Shakespeare canon. We accept unblinkingly the differences between the early history plays on Henry VI and the Plautine and romantic comedies which immediately preceded and followed them. We raise no critical or theatrical-historical eyebrow at the gross stylistic disparities between Globe plays such as *Hamlet* or *Julius*

Caesar and the three golden comedies, all written at about the
same time, nor suggest a change in playing conditions or
audiences to explain the dramatist's abrupt shift in manner and
method. Dowden's biographical fantasies about Shakespeare'
being on the heights and in the depths are no longer taken seriously. Instead, we accept the fact that Shakespeare, a great
creative artist as well as a professional playwright, tried his
hand at many genres, and kept up with, if he did not lead the
way in, rapidly changing theatrical fashions.

Richard Hosley has stated his belief that the Swan Playhouse,
as recorded in the famous De Witt drawing, "is not only typical
of Elizabethan public playhouses but is also capable of accom-
modating the production of nearly all extant Elizabethan
plays."[16] We are gradually coming to see that the specific
physical features of Elizabethan and Jacobean playhouses were
less important to the companies, and therefore less influential
on the playwrights' dramaturgy, than we once believed. Not
long ago the inner stage was thought to be a permanent feature
of every Elizabethan public playhouse, and to be absolutely
essential for the production of many plays. Both views are now
known to be false. It is probably equally erroneous and un-
warranted to give undue emphasis to the physical features of
the Blackfriars as having had a major impact on Shakespeare's
style.

Like anything else, the drama evolved, and fashions changed,
but that there was a much greater uniformity of theatrical taste
and production methods within periods of a few years than
Harbage, Bentley and their followers would have us believe,
is becoming apparent. This claim has recently been made most
provocatively by Glynne Wickham, who points out that

> Only madmen would deliberately prepare for court performances
> in conditions totally different from those at court. For not only
> would every move have to be reblocked to meet radically different
> stage and scenic conditions, but the loss of income to companies
> better prepared would be too serious to contemplate.[17]

He concludes that "after 1597 any playhouse licensed and
built for 'public playing' must have borne a close relationship

[16] Richard Hosley, "The Origins of the So-called Elizabethan Multiple Stage,"
The Drama Review, XII (1968), 28.
[17] Wickham, "The Privy Council Order," p. 44.

n its stage and scenic devices to conditions of performance normal at court." But even if Shakespeare wrote his last plays with half an eye on the possibility of their ultimate performance at court, there is one other factor that should be mentioned. Virginia Woolf, while nervously awaiting the publication of *To the Lighthouse* in 1927, wrote in her diary:

> For the truth is I feel the need of an escapade after these serious poetic experimental books whose form is always so closely consider-ed. I want to kick up my heels and be off. I want to embody all those innumerable little ideas and tiny stories which flash into my mind at all seasons. I think this will be great fun to write; and it will rest my head before starting the very serious, mystical poetical work which I want to come next.[18]

Obviously Shakespeare was no Bloomsbury liberal, and his plays were written under pressure and for money, but it can hardly be denied, although it is sometimes convenient for the sake of argument to forget, that he was also a self-conscious artist, craftsman and poet. In considering the last plays of the greatest writer in English, we should concede the possibility that, like Virginia Woolf, he may have had an interest, not only in con-tent, but also in style and form.

[18] Virginia Woolf, *A Writer's Diary*, ed. Leonard Woolf (London, 1953), p. 105.

Romance and Emblem:
A Study in the Dramatic
Structure of
The Winter's Tale

GLYNNE WICKHAM

It is striking that the drama which arose in England and in Spain during the closing decades of the sixteenth century has gained the lasting respect of posterity, while no such phenomenon occurred in other countries at that time.

Those who have had cause to reflect upon this point may also have been struck by the paradox implicit in the coupling of England and Spain in this context at this particular time; for in so many other ways it would seem more natural for England to have been coupled with Germany, and Spain with Italy. With Spain universally recognized as the champion of Catholicism in the latter half of the sixteenth century, and England no less famous (or infamous) as the bastion of Protestant aspirations, that unity of purpose which had been aimed at by Henry VII at the start of the century when marrying Prince Arthur and, following Arthur's death, Prince Henry to Catherine of Aragon was briefly reaffirmed in the marriage of their daughter Mary to Philip of Spain; but with the accession of Elizabeth on Mary's death in 1558 it evaporated again. In an age when religion was inseparable from politics this difference of creed, and more especially the excommunication of Elizabeth in 1570, sufficed to place the two countries in opposing camps as bitter enemies, and to carry neighbouring Scotland (which Henry VII had also linked to the English crown by marrying his daughter Margaret to James IV) into that of the enemy.

THE GREAT STAGE OF THE WORLD

PLATE 1   *Theatre Collection, Bristol University*

Setting by Anthony Rowe for Calderón's *The Great Theatre of the World*, presented by students of the Bristol Old Vic Theatre School in the Vandyck Theatre, University of Bristol, 1968, translated and directed by George Brandt.

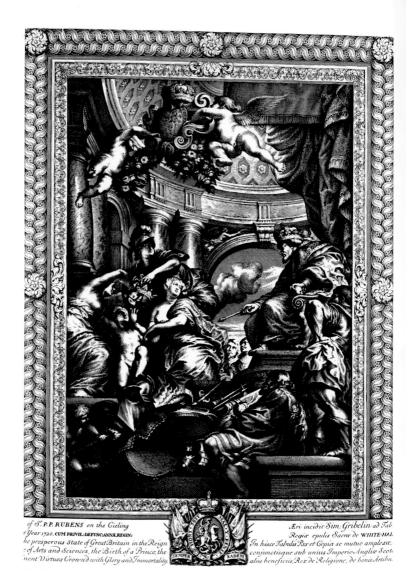

of S^t. P.P. RUBENS on the Cieling   Æri incidit Sim: Gribelin ad Tab
e Year 1720. CUM PRIVIL: DEFUNC ANNÆ REGIN: Regiæ epulis Sacræ de WHITE-HAL
he prosperous State of Great Britain in the Reign   In hisce Tabulis Pax et Copia se mutuo amplexæ,
: of Arts and Sciences, the Birth of a Prince, the   conjunctisque sub unius Imperio Angliæ Scot
nent Virtues Crown'd with Glory and Immortality.   aliis beneficiis, Rex de Religione, de bonis Artibu.

PLATE 2

Opposite: Engraving by Simon Gribelin, 1720, of a panel in the ceiling of Inigo Jones' Banqueting House, Whitehall, commissioned from Rubens by Charles I and installed as a memorial to his father, James I. The panel is one of the two rectangular paintings flanking the Apotheosis of James I and depicts the Union as an infant identifiable by means of the armorial shield in the top left-hand corner in which the Arms of the King of Scotland are crossed with those of the King of England. Britannia is depicted in the act of crowning the child (the United Kingdom) in the presence of King James. Prince Charles and the Duke of Buckingham are included as spectators in the background.

PLATE 3
Portrait of Prince Henry at the time of his Investiture as Prince of Wales, attributed to Robert Peake.

National Portrait Gallery

PLATE 4

Inigo Jones' design for the costume worn by Prince Charles as Zephirus in Samuel Daniel's Investiture Mask, *Tethys' Festival*, June, 1610.

PLATE 5   *Westminster Abbey*

Wax effigy (from the death-mask) of Henry VII made for his funeral, 1509.

PLATE 6 *National Portrait Gallery*

Elizabeth, wife of Henry VII, holding the white rose of York. Painting by an unknown artist.

PLATE 7

Marble effigy of Queen Elizabeth I commissioned by James I and executed by Cornelius Cure, 1606, at a cost of £765. It lies above her tomb in the North aisle of the Henry VII Chapel in Westminster Abbey.

Eric de Maré

PLATE 8   *Kerry Dundas*

The marble effigy of Mary, Queen of Scots, commissioned by James I
and carved by Cornelius and William Cure, 1607-12, at a cost of more
than £1,000. It lies above her tomb in the South aisle of the Henry VII
Chapel in Westminster Abbey.

One immediate consequence in England was the total suppression of religious drama in the course of the next decade and the imposition of a tough censorship upon all plays, culminating in the establishment of the Licensing Commission of 1589. With the execution of Mary, Queen of Scots, on English soil in 1587, Protestant relations with the Catholic world reached their nadir, and those between England and Scotland descended to a point in Scottish eyes seemingly past forgiving or forgetting.

By contrast, Spanish drama progressed smoothly during these years of storm and stress. Having been purged already by Torquemada at the end of the fifteenth century, no new censorship descended on Iberian stages either before or after the defeat of the Invincible Armada in 1588.

Yet despite these differences—religious, political and social— in the historical development of the two countries in the late sixteenth century, the drama blossomed in both as it had never done before and in a manner unique to Europe at that time. Why?

Such a question, if it is to be fully answered, demands a much more intimate knowledge of linguistic, literary, artistic and social conditions in Spain than I possess; but at least a partial answer is to be found once it is realized that in these two countries alone the gothic tradition of typological, prefigurative and emblematic methods of play-construction survived virtually intact, absorbing en route such new ideas common to the age as were useful.

In Germany and the Low Countries, as we are well aware, perpetual wars disrupted and delayed the development of dramatic art at this time. We know, by contrast, that in Italy first and then in France courtly society turned its back on the gothic past, dismissed it as barbarous, and entered eagerly upon a phase of academic antiquarianism in playwriting and theatrical representation. However, we also know that in England and in Spain, despite the inroads of Renaissance pressures of dramatic theory and practice upon earlier traditions, much stiffer opposition was encountered from within the theatre itself because of its fast-growing professionalism and much less lavish and well-organized support from court and academic patrons.

In the theatre these differences of outlook resulted in a steadily expanding literary drama dominated by the poets, and in a steadily increasing professionalism in presentation dominated by the leading actors. A logical development of these tendencies in the late sixteenth and early seventeenth centuries was the merging of the two in the actor-playwright-director or the manager-playwright-director. Men of this ilk emerged in Spain, in Lope de Vega and Calderón; in England, in Jonson, Heywood, Shakespeare and D'Avenant. By temperament and education such men were open to the new ideas of the time; by profession they were immersed in the projection of ideas to the public at large by rhetorical means; by good fortune they enjoyed the protection of powerful patrons. From this enviable position of strength they were able to secure for the popular theatre a form of management that was at once coherent yet flexible, conservative yet progressive, and thus able to speak simultaneously to courtier, to peasant and to artisan.

This professional self-reliance of actors and play-makers in Spain and England is reflected in their theatres, which were adjustable enough to contain a wide variety of types of entertainment ranging from bear-baiting, cock-fighting and sword fights to acrobatics, dances, and secular and religious stage plays; it is reflected in the easy trafficking of the actors between public amphitheatres, provincial town halls and banquet-hall stages in royal palaces; it is reflected in their personal commissions. Calderón as Master of the Revels to King Philip IV, Jonson as Poet Laureate to James I, and Shakespeare as principal play-maker to the King's own company of actors from 1603 to 1616, share in common this ability to represent the views of their masters in emblematic form in the forum of the public theatres and to carry back to their masters, within similar dramatic emblems, some indication of the tastes and interests of their subjects. Censorship in both countries was strict; but author, leading actor and manager, having once obtained a licence to present a play, were then free to rehearse and direct it as they pleased, and the copyright lay vested in the company. In these conditions the emblematic play was better suited than any other to professional actors trafficking between palace and public playhouse.

II

To such men as these the emblematic play was not simply a style and form of dramatic composition inherited from the past which could be copied, but a vehicle which, because its form resembled that of a riddle, enabled them to discuss religious, political and social issues notwithstanding the censorship.

An emblematic play is not an allegory, nor is it a parable; it is a dramatic narrative in the course of which allusion is made, more or less frequently but always obliquely, to other characters and another story or stories. It often takes the form of a romance into which references to factual matters of a topical nature have been inserted. On the stage, therefore, what meets the eye and ear is likely to differ greatly from what the author and the actors are projecting at the minds of their audience; for what reaches their understanding usually takes the form of moral or political instruction, while the outward shape of the play is purely pleasurable and entertaining. Interpretation of the emblem is thus a matter for the discerning spectator.

The quest for naturalism in dramatic writing in more modern times and for pictorial realism in theatrical representation has made us neglectful if not contemptuous of this older, emblematic form of composition. More seriously, it has blinded many men of letters, especially critics of Elizabethan drama, to the fact that it ever existed.

Critics of Spanish drama have served the authors of their golden age better, in this respect, than those of the English-speaking world have served Shakespeare and his contemporaries. Nevertheless, it took a performance of Calderón's *El Gran Teatro del Mundo* by students of the Bristol Old Vic Theatre School in 1968 to awaken me to the actual mechanics of an emblematic play in action on the stage, and to lead me to suppose that those correspondences between dramatic fictions and historical actualities that figure so frequently in Shakespeare's plays might be more than accidental. Not all of Calderón's plays are emblematic, but *The Great Theatre of the World* is explicity so in its very title (Plate 1). The lesson learned from this production was one that I begin to apply to several Elizabethan and Jacobean plays. It struck me at once that plays like Middleton's notorious *A Game At Chess*, Jonson and Nashe's *The Isle of Dogs*, and Chapman's "Biron" plays, all of which caused embarrassment to the government of the day, might well have done so because the political moral was too obtrusive. And if these plays were emblematic in construction (as *A Game At Chess* unquestionably is), then the possibility that some of the structural features which have puzzled critics of Shakespeare's

85

plays, particularly the later ones, might well admit of similar explanation.

Shakespeare's concern with the major issues of domestic and foreign policy is, to my mind, already evident in such relatively early plays as *Romeo and Juliet* and the histories. These are not emblematic plays, but they are more than dramatized romances; they do ask serious political questions. Are Scotland and England, Catholics and Protestants, forever to be divided because one bad deed deserves another? Is the prospect of a smooth succession and the ultimate union of the two countries to be wrecked by a revenge ethic that goes back to the battle of Flodden in 1513 and the rejection of papal supremacy in 1537, and which will forever demand an eye for an eye and a tooth for a tooth in the retributive manner of Montagues and Capulets, Yorkists and Lancastrians?

Happily, time was to answer this question with a firm no. The accession of James I without a civil war and his survival of the gunpowder plot opened the way to a new ethic in both domestic and foreign politics—the replacement of revenge and retribution for past insults and injuries with conscious attempts to heal old wounds by recourse to mercy, forgiveness and regenerative love. This shift of emphasis in the political affairs of the court and the nation after 1605 is clearly reflected in the drama of the time with the advent of tragi-comedy; in some instances the shift is merely generalized, but in others it is more direct and deliberately emblematic. The keys to the emblems lie in the manipulation of the source material and thus in the construction of such plays.

A case in point was *The Winter's Tale*, a play performed both to public audiences at the Globe and to the nobility at court with apparent success, yet one for which critics from Ben Jonson onwards have felt obliged to apologize because of its loose construction. The correspondence between the double setting in Sicilia and Bohemia, the events depicted in them and the passage of time embraced by the play on the one hand, and the course of Anglo-Scottish relations in the sixteenth century on the other hand, is striking. The happy start initiated by Henry VII in the marriage of his daughter Margaret to James IV, only to be belied by the battle of Flodden (1513) and the execution of Mary, Queen of Scots, at Fotheringay (1587), succeeded by the reunification of these neighbouring kingdoms under

James I (1603), follows, in general outline at least, the same course as that of the plot of *The Winter's Tale*. Both stories possess the essentials of "comic" shape; in both, time is the re-generative factor which transforms a disastrous divorce into the restored harmony of the next century, and the daughter of Time, as is evident from the motto attached to the title page of Robert Greene's *Pandosto*, is Truth.

That such historical correspondences were not simply a myth of twentieth-century hindsight seems proven by Anthony Munday's use of them to frame his Pageants for the Lord Mayor's Show in 1605, *The Triumphs of re-united Britania*; for there he uses the original division of Britain into three Kingdoms by the first Brutus, Henry VII's part in its eventual reunifica-tion, and the equation of James himself with the second Brutus, as the principal thematic material for this first mayoral show of the new reign. Shakespeare, too, made repeated allusions to these historical points in his later plays, notably in *Macbeth*, *King Lear*, *Cymbeline* and *Henry VIII*.

It was on this evidence that I ventured upon a speculative essay, "A Comedy with Deaths," in *Shakespeare's Dramatic Heritage* (London, 1969), drawing attention to these corre-spondences and suggesting that if they were regarded as delibe-rate they might explain the disparate structure of *The Winter's Tale* with its sixteen-year time-gap as essential components of its structure rather than as lazy-minded blunders on the part of an ageing and careless poet. In making this suggestion I had before me Simon Gribelin's engraving of Ruben's depiction of the reunification of the kingdom which Charles I commission-ed as a memorial to his father to adorn the ceiling of Inigo Jones' Banqueting House at Whitehall. This picture and its eight companion panels is as fully emblematic in the domain of the fine arts as Calderón's *El Gran Teatro del Mundo* is in that of the drama (Plate 2). I did not feel, however, on this evi-dence, that I could press the matter further. Before *The Win-ter's Tale* could definitely be designated an emblematic play in the full sense of either the Rubens painting or Calderón's drama, or even Middleton's *A Game At Chess*, further research would have to supply evidence that could both detach the emblem from within the narrative and tie it firmly to the occa-sion of the play's production in 1610. It was a contemporary event, the investiture of H.R.H. Prince Charles as Prince of

Wales in June 1969, that supplied the clue to the direction this research should take: a précis of these findings appeared in *The Times Literary Supplement* of December 18, 1969, under the title of "Shakespeare's Investiture Play: the Subject and Occasion of *The Winter's Tale*." A fuller, more complete account is now given in the final sections of this paper.

III

The claim to be made is that *The Winter's Tale* represents Shakespeare's contribution to the celebrations marking the investiture of Henry Stuart as Prince of Wales and heir apparent to the reunited Kingdoms of England, Wales and Scotland in June 1610. The evidence is drawn from two Pageants by Anthony Munday, two Masques by Ben Jonson, a poem and a Masque by Samuel Daniel, three of James I's own speeches and two statues sculpted by Cornelius and William Cure, master-masons to the King.

King James and the Union

James arrived in London late in 1603 and issued a Proclamation in 1604 declaring the Union of the Crowns accomplished. Parliament, however, refused to accept it as more than an expression of the King's wishes, forcing him to fight for four more years to get them implemented.

James addressed Parliament, in person, no less than three times on this subject. He brought it before his first Parliament (1603) when he told members,

> First, by my Descent lineally out of the Loynes of *Henry* the Seventh, is reunited and confirmed in me the Union of the two princely Roses of the two Houses of LANCASTER and YORKE....

James had already given this thought practical expression in christening his two eldest children Henry and Elizabeth. His address continued,

... but the Union of these two princely Houses is nothing comparable to the Union of the two ancient and famous Kingdoms, which is the other inward Peace annexed to my Person.

(Lord Somers Tracts, 2nd Series, I,147)

The Proclamation followed in 1604, and a sequel was Anthony Munday's Pageant for Lord Mayor's Day, 1605, *The Triumphs of re-united Britania,* in which the whole Brutus legend and. its happy ending in James I's accession was displayed emblematically to public view.

The principal scenic device of the show was "a Mount triangular, as the Island of *Britayne* it selfe is described to bee." Seated on its summit was Britannia, Brutus' wife, "a fayre and beautifull Nymph," together with Brutus himself dressed "in the habite of an adventurous warlike Troyan." The three kingdoms into which Brutus had divided Britain were personified in his three sons, Camber, Albanact and Locrine, who sat below their mother and father in the Pageant: below them sat personifications of the rivers which served as boundaries to the kingdoms. Each in their speeches made their own part in the story explicit to the citizens, but the character with most to say was Brutus. First he reminds his hearers of his marriage and his conquest of the Western Isles.

Then built I my *New Troy,* in memorie
Of whence I came, by *Thamesis* faire side,
And nature giving me posterity,
Three worthy sonnes, not long before I died,
My Kingdome to them three I did devide.
   And as in three parts I had set it downe,
   Each namde his seat, and each did weare a Crowne.

(sig.Biii^r)

After letting them take up their parts of the tale, he resumes his own and invites his audience to turn their minds away from the past and towards the present, "to tell olde Britaines new borne happy day."

That seperation of her sinewed strength,
Weeping so many hundred yeeres of woes
Whereto that learned Barde [i..e. Merlin] dated long length
Before those ulcerd wounds againe could close,

89

And reach unto their former first dispose.
> Hath run his course thorough times sandie glasse,
> And brought the former happines that was.

Albania, Scotland, where my sonne was slaine
And where my follies wretchednes began,
Hath bred another *Brute*, that gives againe
To *Britaine* her first name, he is the man
On whose faire birth our elder wits did scan,
> Which Prophet-like seventh Henry did forsee,
> Of whose faire childe comes *Britaines* unitie.

And what fierce war by no meanes could effect,
To re-unite those sundred lands in one,
The hand of heaven did peacefully elect
By mildest grace, to seat on *Britaines* throne
This second *Brute*, then whome there else was none.
> *Wales, England, Scotland*, severd first by me:
> To knit againe in blessed unity.

(sig.Biii^v)

Brutus then proceeds to expound the emblematic, visual iconography of the Pageant to the citizens watching in the streets.

For this *Britannia* rides in triumph thus,
For this these Sister-kingdomes now shake hands,
Brutes Troy, (now London) lookes most amorous
And stands on tiptoe, telling forraine lands,
So long as Seas beare ships, or shores have sands:
So long shall we in true devotion pray,
And praise high heaven for that most happy day.

(sigs.Biii^v-Biiii^r)

However, continuing English opposition to union with Scotland obliged James to go to Parliament again in 1606 to try to talk it into confirming his Proclamation with a statute.

And therefore now let that which hath been sought so much, and so long, and so often, by Blood and Fire, and by the Sword, now it is brought and wrought by the Hand of God, be embraced and received with an Hallelujah...and let all at last be compounded and united into One Kingdom.

(Journals of the House of Commons, I, 315)

In 1608, very angry, James summoned both Houses of Parliament to Whitehall and harangued them for a third time. At last he got his way, if only in an act that negated earlier, hostile legislation against the Scots.

As a source for his rhetoric James only had to study Daniel's *A Panegyricke Congratulatory* written in 1601 (?) and published both in London and Edinburgh in 1603.

And now she is, and now in peace therefore
Shake hands with Union, O though mighty State,
Now thou art all *Great-Britaine* and no more,
No Scot, no English now, nor no debate;
No borders but the Ocean and the Shore:
. . . .
What heretofore could never yet be wrought
By all the swords of pow'r, by blood, by fire,
By ruine and distruction; here is brought
To passe with peace, with love, with joy, desire:
Our former blessed union hath begot
A greater union that is more intire,
And makes us more our selves, sets us at one
With Nature that ordain'd us to be one.[1]

This work of Daniel's was almost certainly in Munday's hands when he wrote *The Triumphs of re-united Britania* and supplied James with many other ideas relating to the Union and its consequences. James, however, could give in as good measure as he borrowed when it came to images and figures.

Addressing Parliament in 1606 on the benefits of Union, James observed, "I am the husband and all the whole Isle is my wife." This figure, as we shall see, was destined to make a deep impression on Shakespeare's poetic mind.

Prince Henry and the Union

In 1610, with the investiture of the Prince of Wales and heir apparent, the subject again attracted public attention, but in a new guise. On the night of January 6 the whole Henry–Arthur–Brutus legend was aired again at court, this time by Ben Jonson and Inigo

---

[1] *The Complete Works in Verse and Prose*, ed. A. B. Grosart, 5 vols. (London, 1885-96; reprinted New York, 1963), I, 143-44. All quotations from Daniel are taken from this edition.

Jones. The *dramatis personae* of their "Masque at Barriers" were: The Lady of the Lake, Chivalry, Arthur, Merlin and Melia- dus. King Arthur was represented in the form of the star Arcturus; Meliadus was played by Prince Henry himself. The literary and moral focus of the Masque is Merlin's two-hundred- line speech about the glories of British history. (It was to Merlin that the original *Arturus redivivus* prophecy had been attribut- ed.) Jonson reverses James's debt to Daniel and quotes directly from the King's first address to Parliament in 1603.

> Here are kingdomes mixt
> And nations joyn'd, a strength of empire fixt
> Conterminate with heaven; The golden veine
> Of SATURNES age is here broke out againe.
> HENRY but joyn'd the *Roses*, that ensign'd
> Particular families, but this hath joyn'd
> The *Rose* and *Thistle*, and in them combin'd
> A union, that shall never be declined.[2]

A year later, on January 1, 1611, Jonson and Jones are still harping on "the proper heir, Design'd so long to Arthur's crowns and chair," in their *Masque of Oberon*.

The actual investiture took place in the week of May 31 to June 6 (Plate 3). London celebrated it with a water pageant on the Thames. Richard Burbage and John Rice of the King's Men play- ed the parts of Amphion and Corinea, riding respectively on a dolphin "personating the genius of Wales" and a whale "figuring" the Duchy of Cornwall; the text, *London's Love for Prince Henry*, was by Anthony Munday. The dramatic centrepiece, however, was the Court Masque, *Tethys' Festival*, by Samuel Daniel and Inigo Jones, which the Queen (Tethys), Princess Elizabeth (Thames) and Prince Charles (Zephirus) presented to James I (Ocean's King) and Prince Henry (Meliadus). Tethys explains that she and her attendant rivers have recently visited Milford Haven,

> The happy Port of Union, which gave way
> To that great Hero HENRY, and his fleete,
> To make the blest conjunction that begat
> A greater, and more glorious far than that. (III,314)

---

[2] *Ben Jonson*, ed. C. H. Herford, Percy and Evelyn Simpson, 11 vols. (Oxford, 1925-52), VII, 333.

They bring the sword of Justice and the scarf of Mercy (embroidered with a map of Britain) to Prince Henry. In reverting to this imperial theme[3] Daniel elects also to expand Jonson's image of "the golden veine/of SATURNES age" by playing on the word "spring" in its triple sense of river's source, pastoral innocence and vernal fertility. He describes Prince Charles as

Faire branch of power, in whose sweete feature here
Milde Zephirus a figure did present
Of youth and of the spring-time of the yeare. (III, 322)

and makes Tethys instruct him to

Breath out new flowers, which yet were never knowne
Unto the Spring, nor blown
Before this time, to bewtifie the earth. (III,312)

By good fortune the costume designed by Inigo Jones for Prince Charles to wear in this masque has survived (Plate 4).

When Jonson's and Daniel's treatments of the theme of Union in their dramatic celebrations of the investiture and Burbage's willingness to participate are considered, it seems probable that Shakespeare would either choose or be required to make a similar contribution. *Cymbeline*, with its British princess, its two British princes brought out of Wales, and the repeated references to Milford Haven, is a possible candidate. The date fits. I think, however, that Shakespeare went beyond this generalized compliment to the royal children, taking up the two themes already advanced, adding a third, especially dear to the King, and weaving them into a single artistic entity, dramatic and emblematic.

Mary, Queen of Scots, and the Union

It might seem that the investiture consummated the Union, emblematically speaking. In a sense it did; but there was still one dark blot on the new escutcheon—the decapitated corpse of James's mother, executed by order of Elizabeth at Fotheringay in 1587. No rapprochement between Scotsmen and Englishmen,

---

[3] The theme, first expounded by Munday in *The Triumphs of re-united Britania* (1605; see p. 89 above), was expanded by Jonson in his Masque, *The Speeches at Prince Henries Barriers* (1610; see p. 92 above), and again, in its most poetic form, by Shakespeare in *Henry VIII* (V.v.16-56).

Protestants and Catholics, could be complete until this English
wound to Scottish pride had been publicly forgiven. James
took this task of public atonement upon himself. On his accession in 1603, sixteen years after the execution, he furnished
Mary's grave in Peterborough Cathedral with a costly pall. Daniel, in his *Panegyricke Congratulatory*, deals with this problem:

> A King of *England* now most graciouslie,
> Remits the iniuries that have beene done
> T'a King of Scots, and makes his clemencie
> To checke them more then his correction;
> Th' annointed bloud that stain'd most shamefully
> This ill seduced State, he lookes thereon
> With th'eye of griefe, not wrath, t'avenge the same,
> Since th' Authors are extinct that caus'd that shame. (I,153)

It was certainly in this spirit that James himself approached the
problem; but he had a more ambitious plan in mind, and in
realizing it he chose once again to work emblematically, letting
the minds of his subjects deduce the moral of his action from the
evidence presented to their eyes.

The keystone of his thinking was the Henry VII chapel in
Westminster Abbey in the middle of which stood the tomb
of Henry Tudor and Elizabeth of York surmounted by twin effigies, the outward emblems of his own claim to the English
crown (Plates 5 and 6). In 1605 James commissioned his master-
mason, Cornelius Cure, to make two marble statues, one of
Queen Elizabeth and one of Queen Mary. When Cornelius died
in 1607 the statue of Elizabeth was finished but that of Mary
Stuart was not. He was succeeded in office by his son, William,
who received the commission to finish Mary's statue. It took him
and the painter James Muncey nearly four years to do it; but
Cure received £825 for his labours. The King's debts in 1614
included £1,000 for this tomb.[4] On September 28, 1612, James
sent a warrant from Hampton Court to the Dean and Chapter
of Peterborough, a facsimile of which is inscribed on Queen
Mary's tomb in Westminster Abbey:

> Trusty and welbeloved wee greet you well, for that wee thinke it
> appertaynes to the duty wee owe to our dearest Mother that like

[4] B.M. MS. Lansdowne 164, f.387b.

honour should be done to hir body and like Monument be extant of hir, as to others hirs and our Progenitours have beene used to be done and our selves have allready performed to our deare Sister Queen Elizabeth. Wee have commaunded a Memoriall of hir to be made in our Church of Westminster, the place where the Kinges and Queenes of this realme are usually interred. And for that wee thinke it inconvenient that hir Monument and hir Body should be in severall places wee have ordered that hir said Body remayning now interred in that our Cathedral Church of Peterborough shalbe removed to Westminster to hir said Monument.

Arthur Wilson, in his contemporary *History of Great Britain under James I* (1653), recorded of Mary that, on October 8,

... (somewhat suitable to her mind when she was living) she had a translucent passage in the night, through the City of London, by multitudes of torches... attended by many Prelates and Nobles, who payed this last Tribute to her *memory*. This was accounted a *Piaculous action* of the King's.... (p. 61)

This "piaculous action," or deed of atonement, is the third of the three themes publicly associated with the Union. From that day forward Mary and Elizabeth were to lie, and have lain, under their marble statues (alas, now stripped of Mauncey's paint) in the north and south aisles of the Henry VII chapel; and with them, as James profoundly hoped, lay buried all the rancorous contentions about the Protestant bastard and the Catholic whore (Plates 7 and 8). James disassociated himself from Mary and Elizabeth, choosing Henry VII's tomb as his own resting place.[5]

The Cures, father and son, worked for more than four years on Mary's statue and it is unthinkable that this commission, especially after the erection of Elizabeth's statue, was not common knowledge in court circles. Living in the Parish of St. Thomas the Apostle, Southwark, they were neighbours of the King's Men at the Globe and of Shakespeare himself when residing in the Clink. It thus seems just as probable that Shakespeare should not only know of Cure's commission but could witness

---

[5] Because James was buried in this tomb which was already surmounted by two effigies, Charles I had to find some other means of commemorating his father. In the event, he chose to do this not in Westminster Abbey, but in the Banqueting House of his own palace at Westminster (Plate 2).

progress on it at any time he chose between 1606 and 1610, as that he was aware of the examples set by Munday, Jonson and Daniel in giving dramatic life to critical issues of domestic politics in 1610 itself.

The Winter's Tale *and the Investiture*

We know from the Chamber Accounts that the play was among those presented in the spring of 1613 for the wedding of Princess Elizabeth; from the Revels Accounts that it was played at court on November 5, 1611; and from Simon Foreman's *Book of Plaies* that it was seen at the Globe on May 15, 1611. As Sir Henry Herbert tells us that it was first licensed by Sir George Buck, who became Master of the Revels in August 1610, the terminal dates of the first performance must be August 1610 and May 1611.[6] If the play represents Shakespeare's contribution to Prince Henry's investiture, it is one of the fifteen plays which the King's Men presented at court between October 1610 and January 1611 for which, according to the Chamber Accounts, they were paid £150 on February 12, 1611.

All the evidence set out here now combines to designate *The Winter's Tale* as having been written for performance in the autumn of 1610 before the King and the heir-apparent following his investiture as Prince of Wales at the age of sixteen.

IV

So much for the occasion; now for the subject matter. The claim that this play is emblematic in the same full sense as Calderón's *El Gran Teatro del Mundo* and the Rubens ceiling in the Whitehall Banqueting Hall rests in part on the occasion which the play was designed to celebrate and in part on the presence in the text of political moralizing apposite to that occasion injected into the romantic narrative drawn (with important alterations) from Robert Greene's novel *Pandosto*, subtitled "The Triumph of Time."

[6] Buck, who held the reversion of the Office from Tilney from 1603 onwards, started, as Acting Master, to license plays for printing in 1607; but this does not conflict with Herbert's statement nor does it imply that he was also authorizing plays for performance before he became Master in his own right.

If the play was intended to be an allegory, events in the narrative would have to run parallel with those in Anglo-Scottish history, and the *dramatis personae* would have to bear marked resemblances to their historical equivalents. In neither case is this true of *The Winter's Tale*. As an emblem, however, both narrative and characters need do no more than reflect a particular situation; and this *The Winter's Tale* does in a remarkable manner. At its simplest it reflects the surprising, if not miraculous, reunification of the British Isles in the person of the heir-apparent, Prince Henry, followed upon a period of disastrous internecine quarrels culminating in war, imprisonments and deaths.

Essential to this mirror effect is double action in two countries, linked by what Anthony Munday called "times sandie glasse." No less important is the figure provided by King James himself of the relationship between sovereign and kingdom: "I am the husband and all the whole Isle is my wife." Granted this initial image, it is relatively easy to elaborate it in terms of divorce and reunification, of remarriage and of children's inheritance. The basis of the emblematic structure of *The Winter's Tale* is thus Union or Harmony, followed by Divorce, Disintegration or Discord, followed by Reunion and future happiness with Time, Faith and the fulfilment of prophecy as the translating agents. Thus Leontes is to be viewed as three characters: himself at narrative level, the first Brutus in Acts I–III.ii. inclusive, and the second Brutus in Act V. In the last of these three persons only, does he represent James I directly, the wise ruler whose "piaculous actions" have restored "the former happines that was." Hermione is Britain, the wife divorced by the first Brutus and mystically restored to the second. The artistry implicit in borrowing the marble memorials to Elizabeth and Mary, Queen of Scots, from real life and incorporating them into the statue scene in Paulina's chapel, echoing in its dialogue the liturgical drama of the *Visitatio Sepulchri* as the means of effecting this mystical resurrection is dazzling.

Perdita, spoken of by the oracle in prophetic vein as that which is lost and must be found before harmony can be restored, is to be viewed as Reunited Britannia, England and Scotland, Protestant and Catholic, the perfect bride for the new Prince of Wales who, as heir apparent, is destined to incorporate the dragon, the lion and the leopard within a single heraldic escutch-

eon under a single crown—the flower of modern chivalry, Meliadus, Lord of all the Isles, Florizel.

If any other real-life character is personated within the em-
blem it is perhaps Sir Francis Bacon who, as prime architect of
James's efforts to persuade Parliament to accept Anglo-Scottish
Union, resembles Paulina in the play.

> Leontes O grave and good Paulina, the great comfort
> That I have had of thee!
> Paulina   What, sovereign sir,
> I did not well, I meant well.   (V.iii.1-4)

Those with lively imaginations and a taste for romance in
their reading of history may care to see in the Third Gentlemen
of Act V, Scene ii—a "bit part" coveted by all actors worthy of
the name—Shakespeare himself, reverting to his former métier
as actor in order to pay his singular compliment to his fellow
gentlemen usher, master-mason William Cure, in person.

Be that as it may—and it is no more singular than the sixteen-
year time gap between the execution of Mary, Queen of Scots,
and the accession of James I and between the birth of Prince
Henry and his investiture—there is now a strong case for regarding the curious structure of *The Winter's Tale* as having been
deliberately engineered to contain an emblematic device. As
such it is a drama which is comic in form, notwithstanding
three deaths, and one which figures the mystical marriage of
Prince Henry (Florizel) to the Kingdom whose original unity
was lost (Hermione) by the actions of the first Brutus (Leontes
I), but has been found (Perdita) as was prophesied in the fulfilment of Time, thanks to the advent of the second Brutus and
the "piaculous actions" which have now atoned for past mis-
takes (Leontes II: James I). Thus Shakespeare, by substituting
the living statue of Hermione in his own play for the dead
queen of Greene's novel, succeeded in creating a work of art
which was as effective an emblem for his court audience as it
was an enjoyable dramatic romance for his wider public in the
city of London.

It has been a commonplace of literary criticism for a long
time that all masques were emblematic. Prepared to celebrate
an occasion, they automatically reflected in their subject matter
the occasion they were designed to celebrate. From Jonson's

Masque of Blackness to Milton's *Comus*, structure and occasion thus go hand in hand. Critics have drawn attention no less frequently to the influence of masques on Shakespeare's later plays; but only very recently have they begun to recognize that the principal aspect of this influence on plays may lie in the emblematic quality of a play's construction. If *The Winter's Tale* follows the example of masques in celebrating a particular occasion, other plays like *Macbeth, Catiline, Philaster* or *Cymbeline* can still be emblematic in a broader sense as figuring major issues of foreign policy and domestic concern in a manner that instructs without loss of entertainment. This was a technique formulated in the typological religious drama of the Middle Ages, refined and condensed through Renaissance iconography and emblem books in the Tudor interlude, and brought to its triumphant zenith, with or without Italian and Spanish example, in Elizabethan and Jacobean dramaturgy.

If this argument can now be accepted, we have in *The Winter's Tale* a work of art directly comparable with Rubens' idealization of the Union, commissioned by Charles I in memory of his father for the ceiling of the Banqueting House in Whitehall in 1626. Political didacticism informs composition and construction in picture and play respectively; but such is the mastery of style and technique that in each case the diagrammatic moralizing of the moment is transcended by the enduring artistry of the entire work. Yet the structure of the work remains rooted in the events it celebrates.

The Politics of Scholarship:
A Dramatic Comment on the
Autocracy of Charles I

W. R. GAIR

The central incident in the main plot of Shackerly Marmion's *The Antiquary* occurs when Veterano, the antiquarian of the title, is told that

> the duke has been inform'd of your rarieties; and holding them an unfit treasure for a private man to possess, he hath sent his mandamus to take them from you.[1]

This news has a traumatic effect upon Veterano:

> I am struck with a sudden sickness: some good man help to keep my soul in, that is rushing from me, and will by no means be intreated to continue![2]

Marmion's plays seem to be constructed around one central and sensational incident which gives meaning and purpose to the whole dramatic context. In *The Antiquary* this central incident probably had a powerful emotive effect upon the contemporary audience and can best be understood by us in terms of the history of the Elizabethan Society of Antiquaries.

On May 22, 1561, the Lutheran theologian and church his-

---

[1] "The Antiquary," *Dodsley's Old Plays*, ed. W. C. Hazlitt (London, 1874-76), XIII, 479.
[2] *Ibid.*

torian, Flacius Illyricus, wrote to the Archbishop of Canterbury, Matthew Parker, to recommend that

> all manuscript books, including those which are considered to be somewhat rare, as well as those of which even the names are unknown, should be brought out of more remote and obscure places and be put into safer and better known localities.[3]

He was, however, preaching to the converted. Parker was a zealous bibliophile, an ardent antiquarian and a collector of ancient manuscripts, but his concern for these antiquities was not entirely disinterested. Like Cecil he was concerned that the dissolution of the monasteries had caused the dispersal of the ancient libraries of the kingdom and that no adequate provision had been made for the preservation of ancient writings.

It is true that, during the earliest phase of the Reformation in England, John Leyland was authorized by Henry VIII, in 1533,

> to serche and peruse the Libraries of hys realme in monasteries, conentes, and colleges, before their utter destruccyon, whyche God then appoynted for their wyckednesses sake,[4]

but he was quite unable to prevent the wholesale dispersal of these libraries.

> A great nombre of them whych purchased those superstycyous mansyons, reserved of those lybrarye bokes, some to serve theyr inkes, some to scoure theyr candelstyckes, and some to rubbe their bootes. Some they solde to the grossers and sope sellers, and some they sent over see to the bokebynders, not in small nombre, but at tymes whole shyppes full, to the wonderynge of the foren nacyons. (sig.Bi.)

Leyland spent six years travelling throughout England to collect information, not merely about ancient manuscripts but also

---

[3] Parker, *Correspondence* (1573-75) ed. J. Bruce (Cambridge, 1853), p. 140: "ex locis remotioribus et ignobilioribus, in certa quaedam et illustriora comportarentur, omnes libri manuscripti et qui rariores esse existimarentur, aut etiam quorum nomina plane ignorarentur."
[4] John Leylande, *A Laboryous Journey*, ed. J. Bale (London, 1549), sig. Bviii (unsigned)—Bale's note.

about the topography and geography of the land, and unless he is grossly exaggerating when he claims that

> there is almost neyther cape nor baye, haven, creke or pere, ryver or confluence of ryvers, breches, washes, lakes, meres, fenny waters, mountaynes, valleys, mores, hethes, forestes, woodes, cyties, burges, castels, pryncypall manor places, monasteryes, and colleges, but I have sceane them,[5]

his intention was to compile a sixteenth-century version of *Domesday*, a *Liber de Topographia Britannicae Primae*.[6] From this original intention, only the *Prolegomena*, edited with explanatory comment by John Bale in 1549, survives. In it Bale cites a letter of 1546 from an unnamed correspondent, who declares that

> Maistre Leylande ... is in suche a frenesy at thys present, that lytle hope I have of hys recover,[7]

and, as Bale points out, the case was hopeless, for

> I muche do feare it that he ... had a poetycall wytt, which I lament, for I judge it one of the chefest thynges that caused hym to fall besydes hys ryghte dyscernynges. (sig.Biiii.)

Leyland, Bale, Parker and Cecil were conscious that if all the manuscript records of the kingdom were destroyed the task of finding precedents for political or religious decisions would be gravely imperilled, and also that if manuscripts were allowed to remain in private hands subversive doctrines might be propagated. As Bale makes clear, one of the primary reasons why Leyland collected ancient documents was so that

> men myghte by them inveye agaynste the false doctryne of pappistes, corruptynge both the scriptures of God and the chronycles of thys realme, by execrable lyest fables.[8]

There was, too, a nationalistic feeling in the motivation of these

---

[5] *Ibid.* sigs. Diiii/Diiii^V Leylande's own words.
[6] *Ibid.* sig. Diiii^V.
[7] *Ibid.*, sig. Biii^V.
[8] *Ibid.* sigs. Cvi^V/Cvii (unsigned).

early antiquaries; they sought to publish ancient English authors,

> that their wytte workes myghte come to lyght and be spredde
> abroade to the whorthye fame of the land. For by them maye it wele
> apeare, the tymes alwayes consydered, that we are no Barbarouse
> nacyon.[9]

Similarly, Parker was involved in a scholarly form of nationalism, for he was seeking to establish that the church in England had an origin independent of Rome;[10] to have any hope of establishing a case, the ancient records of the kingdom were vital.

Parker corresponded for some years with Bale, Cecil, Stow, Lambarde, Illyricus, John Wigand, Matthias Iudex and other scholars, domestic and foreign, in an effort to locate and preserve any manuscripts of which he could obtain information. Illyricus conveyed to Parker Bale's fears that his collection would be dispersed after his death and his desire that a public library should be founded where it might be deposited. Although no library was established, Parker did prevent the dispersal of these manuscripts, but found them disappointing.[11] To his efforts are owed the earliest editions of Aelfric, *The Testimony of Antiquity* (1566); Matthew of Westminster, *Flores historiarum* (1567); *Gildae de excidio et conquestu Britanniae epistola* (1567); Matthew Paris, *Historia maior* (1571); Asser, *Aelfredi regis res gestae* (1574); Thomas Walsingham, *Historia brevis* (1574) and the *Ypodigma Neustriae* (1574).

Strype, in his *Life of Parker*, insists that

> ... in all the books he put forth, he never added anything of his own,
> nor diminished from the copy, but expressed, to a word, everything
> as he found them in the originals. He feared to smooth the wrinkles
> and wipe off the stains of antiquity.[12]

In the next century, Parker's antiquarian successors were to attack the habit of silent editorial emendation or omission. Sir Simonds D'Ewes, in March 1647, received an angry reply from Roger Dodsworth, complaining:

[9] *Ibid.* sig. Cvii (unsigned).
[10] Parker, *Correspondence*, p. 327n.
[11] Parker, *Correspondence*, p. 287.
[12] Strype, *Life of Parker* (London, 1821), II, 501. Strype is citing Parker's Preface

W. R. Gair

> I cannot indure to be told of vast omissions, when I have not left
> out one word that I liked, in any record, in all my life. As for trans-
> cribing Records literatim and verbatim, let them that list under-
> take itt; I disdayne itt.[13]

Parker, however, did offer to "restore" some corrupt parts in
a manuscript which he had borrowed from Cecil; he refrained
from so doing only because Cecil had a copyist equally able to
supply the deficiencies.[14] The Privy Council was sufficiently
persuaded of the importance of Parker's work to give his efforts
quasi-official recognition, and in 1563 he was authorized to
require private owners of manuscripts to allow him access to
their libraries:

> ... so as both when any need shall require resort may be made for the
> testimony that may be found in them, and also by conference of
> them, the antiquity of the state of these countries may be restored
> to the knowledge of the world.[15]

The result of Parker's research was his *De Antiquitate Britannicae Ecclesiae* (1572) in which he attempted to establish, from
manuscript authority, that the Church in England was founded
upon direct apostolic descent, distinct from the Church in Rome.

It was at about the time this treatise was in press that Parker
was held to have become the first President and Patron of the
Society of Antiquaries. This may, however, be a subsequent
scholarly assumption based upon Parker's known antiquarian
interests, his correspondence with other scholars in the field
and his habit of employing antiquarians in his personal ser-
vice; Jocelinus was his Latin secretary. Whether or not Parker

to his edition of *Asser* (1574). Parker appears to have made a distinction between
supplying missing portions of incomplete manuscripts by transcription from
perfect copies, which was his habitual practice (Strype, II, 511), and emending
apparently corrupt readings without the authority of another copy. These principles do not, however, appear to have been applied with rigour, and speculative
emendation does occur (cf. *Matthew Paris*, ed. Sir L. Madden, *Historia
Anglorum*, Rolls Ser., London, 1866, I, xxxv); it is possible that Parker was de-
ceived by his editors and printers, but he was not always aware which manuscript provided the best text.

[13] *Autobiography and Correspondence of Sir Simonds D'Ewes*, ed. J. O. Halliwell, II (London, 1845), 312.
[14] Parker, *Correspondence*, p. 253.
[15] *Ibid.*, p. 327n.

had a formal relationship to an Antiquarian Society, he was succeeded by Whitgift, who clarified the position by accepting one. Whitgift also followed Parker to the See of Canterbury and inherited his reponsibility for clarifying the ancient status of the Church in England.[16] The first Society of Antiquarians was never contractually chartered by its associates; it grew gradually more formal and more systematically organized as its members and their fame increased. The original fellowship included Stow, Lambarde, Arthur Agarde, Sir William Fleetwood, Sir John Doderidge and Sir James Leigh.[17] Although Whitgift may have remained for some time the official patron of the nascent society, it quickly became secular rather than theological in interest: by the mid 1580s it had established an independent existence. The most distinguished early associate of the Society was William Camden who, in these early years of his career, was at pains to record his indebtedness to the encouragement he received in his historical studies from Sir Philip Sidney;[18] with him was the future translator of the *Britannia*, Philemon Holland. It was this group of scholars who created an organization which gradually became the nearest approximation in Elizabethan England to an academy.

The antiquaries fixed their meeting place at Darby House in the Herald's Office, because the Garter, Sir William Dethicke, was one of their associates.

The Society increased daily; many persons of great worth, as well noble as other learned, joyning themselves unto it.[19]

Launcelot Andrewes, Sir Henry Spelman, Sir Robert Cotton, Sir John Davies, were all accepted as members during the succeeding years and, in 1598, by Camden's introduction, Richard Carew of Anthony was elected a fellow while in London as parliamentary representative for Mitchell in Cornwall.[20] They

[16] Sir William Fleetwood to Sir Thomas Heneage, c. 1580. (Master's *History of the College of Corpus Christi* [Cambridge, 1753], App., xxix, p. 51.)
[17] cf. T. Hearne, *Curious Discourses*, 2nd. ed., II (London, 1771), 421ff.
[18] "ad Lectorem," appended (p. 1) to the 5th ed. of Camden's *Britannia* (London, 1600).
[19] *Reliquiae Spelmannianae*, ed. E. Gibson (Oxford, 1698), p. 69. (Preface to *The Original of the Four Terms of the Year*).
[20] *Survey of Cornwall*, ed. F. E. Halliday (London, 1953), p. 38. The information as to Carew's election appears on his memorial tablet.

met each Friday afternoon during term, subject to formal rules of procedure. They were summoned individually to attend.

Society of Antiquaries to Dr. Stowe.

The place appointed for a Conference upon the question followinge, ys att Dr. Garters house on *Frydaye* the ii of this *November*, being Alsoules day [Nov. 2, 1598], at ii of the clocke in thafternoone, where your opinion in wrytinge or otherwyse is expected. The question is, Of the Antiquitie, Etimologie and privileges of parishes in Englande.[21]

The "opinions" were filed in the society archives: at first a secretary, perhaps Agarde, may have summarized them: later it became the rule for the society to retain holograph copies from each individual. It was an agreed rule of procedure that "in a question which cannot be proved by authoritie probabilities and coniectures are to be used."[22] Unlike the works of other gentlemen, the reports of the antiquaries rarely circulated in manuscript outside the society's membership. Obviously the subjects were of a specialized interest, but it seems to have been a deliberate policy—probably owing to concern lest there be political repercussions—to keep discussions secret until they were printed. The antiquaries were jealous of their privileges; strangers were not admitted to their meetings.

Yt is desired, that you bringe none other with you nor geve anie notice unto anie, but such as have the like sumouns[23]

was the terse instruction on the reverse of the summons to the "conference." The Antiquaries soon gained recognition as an influential corporate body. In 1592, Nashe felt compelled to issue a denial that in *Pierce Pennilesse* he had had any intention of denigrating the study of antiquities; some hostile critics had, it appears, attempted to persuade the Antiquaries that Nashe's attack on Gabriel Harvey's pedantry was a slight upon historical scholarship itself.

[21] Hearne, *Curious Discourses*. These are a transcription of the "opinions" presented to the Society, in *MS. Cotton, Faust. E.V.* This MS., after the break-up of the society, came into the hands of Camden who deposited it in Cotton's library. The summons to Stowe occurs in *MS Ashmolean*, No. lxxxvii (Hearne, I, XV).
[22] *MS. Cotton, Faust. E.V.*, f. 101. These are holographs, dating mainly 1590-1605.
[23] Hearne, I, xv. The summons was addressed to Mr. Bowyer.

The Antiquaries are offended without cause, thinking I goe about to detract from that excellent profession, when (God is my witnesse) I reverence it as much as any of them all, and had no manner of allusion to them that stumble at it. I hope they wil give me leave to think there be fooles of that Art as well as of al other; but to say I utterly condemne it as an unfruitfull studie or seeme to despise the excellent qualified partes of it, is a most false and iniurious surmise.[24]

As the membership increased, so the organization grew more complex. By the end of Elizabeth's reign it was the custom to control meetings by two "moderators" chosen from among the members: in February 1601, these were Sir James Leigh and Francis Tate; in May, Tate and a Mr. Broughton.[25] The moderators probably served a limited term in office, one being replaced at a time to ensure continuity of procedure, and performed the duties of Chairman and Secretary. They may also have had some responsibility for maintaining correspondence with country members, one of whom seems to have been—at least in a casual way—Lord William Howard.[26] Living at Naworth Castle on the Scottish borders, Howard was an active antiquary and used to add to his library by exchanging books, sent from London, for such stones as he found with Latin inscriptions. He tempted Cotton—whose son, Thomas, had married one of his daughters—to visit him in August 1608, with the promise: "I have gotten and know weare to have heere about me at least 12 stones, most of them faire inscriptions that you have not yett heard of. . . ."[27] Another member of his household, Nicholas Roscarrock, shared his interests and may also have had some distant connection with the London Society. Richard Carew who, despite the dissolution of Parliament in February 1598, probably remained in London to attend an antiquaries' meeting

[24] *The Works of Thomas Nashe*, ed. R. B. McKerrow (London, 1910), I, 154. (The Author to The Printer.)
[25] *Cotton, Faust. E.V.*, f. 108.
[26] H. R. Steeves (*Learned Societies and English Literary Scholarship* [New York, 1913], p. 32) points out that a MS. of doubtful authenticity, the West MS. [of c. 1625], lists Henry Howard, Earl of Northampton, as a member as well as Sir Philip Sidney. It is very doubtful whether this is to be credited, but at least it reflects a contemporary opinion that Sidney was associated with academies in the European sense; perhaps it is a confusion with his own informal society, the Areopagus.
[27] *Selections from the Household Books of...Naworth Castle*, ed. G. Ornsby, Surtees Soc. (London, 1878), 412; and cf. D. Mathew, *The Age of Charles I* (London, 1951), p. 299.

in November to which he was summoned, contributed a paper for the November 20 meeting in the following year. This paper, "Of the Antiquity, Variety, and Etimology of Measuring Land in Cornwayl," was, in all probability, sent to be read and not presented in person.[28]

The existence of the Society of Antiquaries was not officially recognized by the Privy Council, but its resources were used by them for political purposes. In 1600 Cotton, perhaps acting as society spokesman, wrote, at the Queen's command, "A brief abstract of the question of precedencie between England and Spaine" in order to adjudicate a dispute which had arisen between Sir Henry Nevile, Ambassador to France, and the Spanish Ambassador, who were discussing an Anglo-Spanish treaty at Calais; he decided in favour of his fellow-country-man.[29] On November 25, 1602, Henry Howard, Lord North-ampton, asked Cotton personally to supply a list of precedents relating to the office of the Earl Marshal.[30] William Lambarde was appointed Keeper of the Records in the Tower in 1602 and on August 4 he presented the Queen with a catalogue of the holdings. While reading it aloud, Elizabeth paused from time to time to ask the meaning of technical terms and, reaching the reign of Richard II, exclaimed, "I am Richard II, know ye not that?"—to which Lambarde replied,

> Such a wicked imagination was determined and attempted by a most unkind Gentleman [Essex] the most adorned creature that ever your Majestie made.

Elizabeth could not resist amplifying the analogy:

> He that will forget God, will also forget his benefactors; this tragedy [Shakespeare's *Richard II*] was played 40tie times in open streets and houses.[31]

The work of the antiquaries was by no means free from political implication and Elizabeth, although personally well-disposed towards them, was not unaware of the dangerous precedents in which they dealt, of which even the most ancient could be relevant to current constitutional crises.

[28] *Survey*, ed. Halliday, p. 39.
[29] *Cottoni Posthuma*, ed. J. Howell (London, 1672), pp. 71-89.
[30] *C.S.P. Dom. (1601-03)*, p. 266.
[31] Lambarde succeeded Heneage as Keeper of the Tower records. The audi-

It was during these last years of Elizabeth's reign that the Society of Antiquaries felt themselves so well constituted and with such distinguished membership that they submitted a request to be granted a royal charter of incorporation. The leading instigators were Cotton, Leigh and Doderidge. They suggested that Elizabeth should found, but not endow, a national deposit library under the supervision of "The Accademye for the Study of Antiquity and Historye founded by Queen Elizabethe," which was to provide a governor and two guardians (no doubt moderators "writ large") to be chosen annually from the academy, or rather the incorporated Society of Antiquaries.[32] The Antiquaries stressed that England ought to emulate the example of continental Europe:

> In foreyn countries whear most civility and learning is their is great regard had of the cherishing and encrease of this kinde of learning [i.e. the study of history and antiquities]: by publicke lectures appoynted for that purpose and their ar erected publick librar">es and accademyes in Germany Italy and ffrance to that end.

For a time it seemed possible that the scheme desired by Parker, Bale and Illyricus would succeed but, although it was pointed out that this library would create a body of national archives where not only ancient manuscripts but also official proclamations might be consulted, Elizabeth, apparently, made no response. This was not, of course, the first proposal to found a national library. In January 1556, John Dee, the scientist and astrologer, had addressed a similar petition to Queen Mary and that of the Antiquaries to her sister was based upon it. Dee suggested the appointment of a commission to determine what manuscripts existed in the kingdom, with the power to compel their owners to allow them to be copied:

> Whereby your Highness shall have a most notable library, learning wonderfully be advanced, the passing excellent works of our forefathers from rot and worms preserved, and also hereafter continually

ence is described by Nichols (*Progresses*, III, 552); Lambarde died only a fortnight after the meeting.
[32] The actual petition is not extant, but the draft outline and "Reasons to move the furdrance of this Corporation" are printed by E. Flugel, *Anglia*, XXXII (1909), 265-8 (from *MS. Cotton, Faust. E.V.*, ff. 89-90).

the whole realm may . . . use and enjoy the whole incomparable treasure so preserved.[33]

But neither Mary nor Elizabeth was anxious for ancient precedents to be freely available for consultation. Because Queen
Mary ignored Dee's petition, he built up his own library which,
by 1583, had grown to some four thousand volumes. He made
his collection available to his pupils, who included Sidney and
Dyer. Dee's library scheme, as well as that of the Society of
Antiquaries, prefigures the foundation of the British Museum
and the appointment of The Historical Manuscripts Commission. Since Dee built up his own library because a national one
was not to be founded, Cotton may well have been similarly
influenced: as Dee's pupils met at his library, so the antiquaries
were to meet at Cotton's.[34]

The antiquaries hoped that a new sovereign of known scholarly interests might welcome the idea of an academy, but they
had to reckon with James's suspicion of any private group which
could exert political influence. Ironically, the Society of
Antiquaries presented for the Stuart government that danger
which Parker and Cecil had been attempting to avert, the political threat represented by ancient documents remaining in
private hands. One of Parker's motives in founding the Society
was probably to ensure that early records were kept in respons-
ible hands, but now in the new reign the members were themselves politically suspect. It was their most distinguished
country member, Richard Carew of Anthony, who recorded
their disappointment in a letter to Cotton of April 7, 1605:

Sir, I praie you geive me leave to impart unto you my greef, that my so
remote dwelling depriveth mee of your sweet and respected Anti-
quarum society, into which your kyndenesse towards mee and
grace with them made mee an Entrance, and unto which (not with-
standing so long discontynuance) my longing desire layeth a Con-
tynuall clayme.

I hearde by my Brother, that in the late Queenes tyme it was lykelie
to have received an establishment and extraordynarie favour
from sundrie great personages: and me thinckes that under so
learned a King this plant should rather growe to his full height, then

---

[33] *Autobiographical Tracts of Dr. John Dee*, ed. J. Crossley, Chetham Soc. (London, 1851), p. 47.
[34] cf. C. F. Smith, *John Dee (1527-1608)* (London, 1909) pp. 15-17.

quaille in the Springe. It importes no little disgrace to our Nation, that others have so many Academyes, and wee none at all, especially seeing wee want not choice of wyttes every waye matcheable with theirs, both for number and sufficyency. Sutch a worcke is worthie of your solicitation and indevour, and you owe yt to your owne fame, and the good of your Countrey.[35]

Carew saw the Society as an embryonic academy, but it could not attain this status without a charter of incorporation: had the proposal to Elizabeth been approved, England would have had the beginnings of a national deposit library (Bodley's, opened in 1602, was a purely private venture) and a Royal Society, some thirty years before France. One infers from Carew's letter that the failure of their attempt to achieve official status led to the gradual decline of the Society, and during the early years of the reign of James their activities as a collective body seem to have ceased; royal disapproval was a strong solvent.

In 1612, Sir Henry Spelman moved from Norfolk to London and took a house in Tuthill Street, Westminster, near to the library of his friend Cotton. Some two years later he attempted to refound the Antiquaries' Society with Cotton, Camden and most of the other surviving members of the original fellowship; they met, once again at the Herald's Office, to agree upon details of procedure. After choosing a Mr. Hackwell to be secretary and deciding "that for avoiding offence, we should neither meddle with matters of State nor of Religion," the meeting was adjourned to consider the question, "Of the Original of Terms."

But before our next meeting, we had notice that his Majesty took a little mislike of our Society: not being enform'd, that we had resolv'd to decline all matters of State.[36]

This new society, which had access to a unique repository of state papers and other documents in Cotton's library, too much resembled a cabal to be tolerated by James's court. This was not, however, the last attempt to set up an antiquarian study group in England before the Interregnum, because in May

[35] *Original Letters of Eminent Literary Men*, ed. Sir H. Ellis, Camden Soc. (London, 1898), pp. 98-99.
[36] *Reliquiae Spelmannianae*, ed. E. Gibson (Oxford, 1698), pp. 69-70. The "Mr. Hackewell" was perhaps George (1578-1649).

W. R. Gair

1638 Sir Edward Dering, who in 1627 had obtained permission from the Council to transcribe manuscripts dating earlier
than the reign of Edward VI, signed an agreement with Sir
Christopher Hatton, William Dugdale and Sir Thomas Shirley.
This Antiquitas Rediviva was, however, rather a contractual
obligation to assist members in each other's research than a
society of the complexity of the earlier institution.[37] Effectively,
therefore, after 1614, historical research had to be carried on
with extreme discretion to avoid any suspicion of a formal
corporate activity which might exert political pressure.

Since the dissolution of the old Society of Antiquaries and the
failure to revive it in 1614, leading scholars, lawyers, politicians,
historians and others—men as varied in their interests as Camden, Spelman, Clarendon, Coke, Jonson, Ussher, Hale and
Hobbes—had been accustomed to use Sir Robert Cotton's
library as a convenient meeting place, but on a casual basis;
as Sir Simonds D'Ewes remarked in May 1625,

> I stepped aside into Sir Robert Cotton's and transcribed what I
> thought good out of some of his manuscripts, or old written books
> in parchement.[38]

Their most learned associate, John Selden, records his gratitude,
in the Dedication to his *Historie of Tithes* (1618), for Cotton's
assistance:

> ...to have borrowed your help, or used that your inestimable Lib-
> rary (which lives in you) assures a curious Diligence in search after
> the inmost, least known and most useful parts of Historicall Truth
> both of Past and Present ages.

The conclusion which, through the resources of Cotton's library,
Selden was able to reach in his examination of tithes was that
they were subject to "lex positiva" alone and not dependent
upon the "Iure Divino"[39]—a result at variance with the Stuart
belief in the powers of the royal prerogative. It was in the reign
of Charles that the resort to ancient precedent became too
important a political weapon to remain a purely scholarly pur-

[37] cf. J. Evans, *A History of the Society of Antiquaries* (Oxford, 1956), p. 21-2.
[38] D'Ewes, *Autobiography*, ed. Halliwell, I, 268-9.
[39] Selden, *Tithes*, Preface, p. xiv.

uit. The work of the antiquary had a direct relevance to the
truggle between Parliament and Crown.

While the scholars who gathered in Cotton's house did
nothing openly to antagonize the Privy Council, they constituted a threat in so far as they were a private body with access to
documents of state. In politics, Cotton was personally indiscreet; in 1615 he lost favour by being involved in the Overbury
murder and the Somerset divorce case.[40]

> For he, being highly esteemed by the Earl of Somerset . . . was ac-
> quainted with this murder by him, a little before it now came to light,
> and had advised him what he took to be the best course for his
> [Somerset's] safety. Sir Robert had his pardon and never came to
> his open trial, yet was in the Christmas holidays of this year commit-
> ted to prison.[41]

He remained jailed for five months until James pardoned the
Earl and Countess of Essex. In May of the following year,
Bolton writing to Camden expressed his

> sorrow that your most esteemed friend, Sir Robert Cotton, hath
> been so unfortunate, as that thereby the common treasure of our
> antiquities, and authentic monuments are barred from wonted
> freedom of access, so that here the fortune of our nation's history
> seems to have set the period of itself.[42]

When Cotton was in disgrace, the authorities reacted by re-
stricting access to his library, thus limiting his political influence. For a time private research and authorized inquiry co-
operated harmoniously and Bishop Ussher, who had been
commissioned by James to describe the antiquities of the
Church in England, wrote to Cotton on December 20, 1624,
to obtain his help in procuring early manuscript records through
the resources of his library.[43] About sixteen months later, however, on April 28, 1626, it was reported to Joseph Mead that

> Sir Robert Cotton's books are threatened to be taken away, because
> he is accused of imparting ancient precedents to the lower house.[44]

[40] cf. F. S. Fussner, *The Historical Revolution* (London, 1962), pp. 119-127.
[41] D'Ewes, *Autobiography*, I, 80.
[42] T. Birch, *The Court and Times of James I* (London, 1848), I, 408.
[43] *Original Letters*, ed. Ellis, p. 131.
[44] T. Birch, *The Court and Times of Charles I* (London, 1848), I, 98.

The threat was not carried out. Only three years later a tract with subversive implications, came to the notice of Lord Wentworth, who informed the Privy Council; in their turn they traced it to Cotton's library. It was a proposal "how a Prince may make himself an absolute tyrant" by abolishing parliaments and ruling by royal fiat on the model of Louis XI. Cotton was arrested, sued in the Star Chamber, and his library sealed. On July 12, 1630, a commission was appointed

> to search what records or other papers of State in the custody of Sir Robert Cotton properly belong to his Majesty, and thereof to certify.[45]

It is likely that Richard James, who was employed by Cotton from about 1625 to catalogue his books and manuscripts, and had, in the previous year, worked with Selden on the examination of the Arundel Marbles, was indiscreet and allowed a circulation and copying of documents from the collection more freely than prudence warranted. The tract did not originate from Cotton's house, as the Attorney General alleged, but had been composed some seventeen years earlier in Florence by Sir Robert Dudley, son to the Earl of Leicester.[46] The Privy Council did not allow this mere inaccuracy to deprive it of an opportunity of silencing a source of authoritative statement on political usage which had been found to be increasingly embarrassing. The result of the affair was, as Simonds D'Ewes rather picturesquely describes it in his *Autobiography*, that

> he [Cotton] would tell me they had broken his heart that had locked up his library from him. I easily guessed the reason, because his honour, and esteem were much impaired by this fatall accident, and his house, that was formerly frequented by great and honourable personages, as well as by learned men of all sorts, remained now [1630] upon the matter desolate and empty. (p. 41)

Cotton died in the following year. The last danger, foreseen by Matthew Parker, in the failure at the Reformation to provide for governmental control of ancient writings of the kingdom had been, for the present, obviated. Cotton's library, where

[45] *C.S.P. Dom. (1629-31)*, p. 89. It is possible that this commission was appointed on the precedent of the allowance granted to Parker in 1568 to have access to private libraries.
[46] D'Ewes, *Autobiography*, III, 42n.

manuscripts of dangerously liberal views could be consulted, was now under royal supervision.

Cotton's son was extremely cautious with his library inheritance. Sir Simonds D'Ewes bitterly complains that Thomas was

> wholly addicted to the tenacious increasing of his worldly wealth, and altogether unworthy to be master of so inestimable a library as his father. For he promised me on Monday, the 16th. day of this month [May, 1631] in the forenoon, when I went to visit him after his father's death . . . that he would lend me some manuscripts I should need for the furthering of the public work I was about; yet ever when I sent to him . . . he put me off with so many frivolous excuses or feigned subterfuges, as I forbore further troubling any messengers. (p. 43)

Thomas had already been compelled to petition the Privy Council to have his father's books and papers restored to him.[47] Had he been warned not to encourage "unauthorized" scholarship?

On D'Ewes' testimony, Cotton, when his library was impounded,

> was so outworn within a few months with anguish and grief, as his face, which had been formerly ruddy and well-coloured . . . was wholly changed into a grim blackish paleness, near to the resemblance and hue of a dead visage.[48]

In his play, Marmion calls Veterano the "great" antiquary but his characterization of him is essentially the same as that popularized by John Earle in *Microcosmographia* (1628)— a comical, unworldly eccentric whose criterion of value was simply antiquity—but Parker would have approved the assertion, "He is of our Religion, because wee say it is most ancient. . . ." Earle unjustly accuses the antiquaries of unreasoning prejudice: "Printed bookes he conteenes, as a novelty of this latter age; but a Manuscript he pores on everlastingly, especially if the cover be all Moth-eaten, and the dust make a Parenthesis between every Syllable"—but, no doubt, there were some who behaved like this and if nothing else, as Earle points out, they achieved a certain tranquillity—"His Grave do's not

---

[47] *C.S.P. Dom. (1629-31)*, p. 89.
[48] D'Ewes, *Autobiography*, II, 41-42.

fright him, for he ha's been us'd to Sepulchers, and hee like Death the better, because it gathers him to his Fathers."

The theme of *The Antiquary* is the commonplace conflict o generations: Lionel, nephew to Veterano, plots to gull hi uncle into allowing him a share of his inheritance before du time. He considers trying to sell him "some stale interludes" by representing them as "some of Terence's hundred anc fifty comedies, That were lost in the Adriatic sea";[49] but insteac he plots to secure the sequestration of his uncle's antiquities Although he is clearly a biased witness, D'Ewes blamec "Richard James, a short red-bearded, high-coloured fellow . . . an atheistical, profane scholar," for the closure of Cotton's library. According to D'Ewes, this James "had so screwec himself into the good opinion of Sir Robert Cotton, as . . . some two or three years before his decease, he bestowed the custody of his whole library on him. James then proceeded to "let out, or lend out Sir Robert Cotton's most precious manu-scripts for money." One of his customers was a certain "Mr. Saint John of Lincoln's Inn," who hired the pamphlet which led to the Star Chamber proceedings.[50]

Marmion's play consistently allows the antiquary to state his case and to argue that his profession is one worthy of ad-miration.

> Did not the Signiory build a state-chamber for antiquities? and 'tis the best thing that e'er they did: they are the registers, the chronicles, of the age they were made in, and speak the truth of history better than a hundred of your printed commentaries. (p.449)

This latter assertion suggests the beginnings of an understand-ing of the value of archaeology. Veterano criticizes the frivol-ity and triviality of the present age, declaring,

> I must reverence and prefer the precedent times before these, which consumed their wits in experiments: and 'twas a virtuous emulation amongst them, that nothing which should profit posterity should perish. (p. 452)

The play does nothing to contradict him. While the figure of the antiquary, as established by Earle, is a comical, eccentric type, what he says must be taken seriously.

[49] *Antiquary*, p. 430.
[50] D'Ewes, *Autobiography*, II, pp. 38-43, passim.

In the fourth act, the threat of the mandamus to his books
and other rarities is lifted, and later the Duke (in disguise) presenting Veterano to Lionel (who is, in turn, disguised as the Duke)
declares:

> This is the famous antiquary I told your grace of, a man worthy your
> grace; the Janus of our age, and treasurer of times passed: a man
> worthy your bounteous favour and kind notice; that as soon forget
> himself in the remembrance of your highness, as any subject you
> have. (p. 519)

Veterano's loyalty to his sovereign and devotion to his country
are not in question, and indeed the Duke hints that the antiquary
may receive political advancement and become a senator.

Marmion's *Holland's Leaguer*, which was first performed in
December 1631, is a play which is well known to have been
produced while a public scandal was taking place. There was
a notorious brothel which overlooked the Globe, Hope and
Swan theatres, built on a mudbank in the Thames, and the
authorities attempted to close it down; but when the Watch
arrived the madame of the establishment, Dona Britanica,

> stands upon her guard, hangs out a *Flagge* of defiance, and bids
> them enter at their peril; they which had a double Armor a good
> cause, and lawful authority, scorning to be outbraved, prepare
> for an assault, she on the other side with her man devill, and her
> she furies, stand to receive them, and to make her triumph more
> glorious, she sets ope the gate, puts downe the *Bridge*, and drawes
> up her *Percullis*, the enemy bravely enters, and comming on in
> good order, they were no sooner on the *Bridge*, and had fil'd it
> from one end to the other, but by a secret device which shee conceal-
> ed downe fell the *Bridge*, and the Corporall and his souldiers were
> halfe drowned in the water.[51]

Marmion exploits this scandal for dramatic effect and, on the
whole, sympathizes with the bawds. Similarly, in *The Antiquary* he is again referring to a contemporary sensation, the
Cotton affair; his sympathies are with the antiquary.

Marmion appears to have been opposed to the autocratic
suppression of Cotton's library and to Charles's plan to con-
fiscate some of Cotton's state papers. Veterano is Cotton's

[51] Nicholas Goodman, *Hollands Leaguer: or an historical discourse of the life of
Dona Britanica Hollandia* (London, 1632), sig. G2.

dramatic paradigm; Veterano's loyalty is not in question
Cotton's study was sealed by November 1629; he died o
May 6, 1631. *The Antiquary* was produced, in all likelihood
between these dates; it belongs probably to late 1629 or earl
1630 and it represents an adverse comment on the autocrati
behaviour of the King and Privy Council. Was it also, lik
Chapman's *Old Joiner of Aldgate*,[52] an attempt to influence
judicial decision of the Star Chamber?

---

[52] cf. W. R. Gair, "La Compagnie des Enfants de St. Paul (1599-1606)," *Drama-turgie et Société* (Paris, 1968), II, 671, and, for a full account of all the details of this incident, see C. J. Sisson, *Lost Plays of Shakespeare's Age* (Cambridge, 1936), pp. 12-79.

The Mannerist Stage
of Comic Detachment

GEORGE R. KERNODLE

When I first studied Shakespeare and Elizabethan drama and a little history of art more than forty years ago, there was no Mannerist age. It had not been invented. In fact, there was no Baroque age that drama and literary historians had heard of. There was, of course, the Renaissance, explained mainly as a revival of the classics, and later a series of classical revivals—Dryden, Pope, and so on—to be interrupted by the romantic revolt of Wordsworth and Coleridge. For a while the eighteenth-century classic age seemed safely defined. But not for long. Soon the classic concept was dangerously undermined by literary borers who traced all kinds of underground connections among *pre*-romantics back to Shakespeare and the Middle Ages. As Shakespeare was the model for Goethe, Victor Hugo and Sir Walter Scott, he must have been *the* great romantic, and Racine only an odd aberration to please Greek scholars at the court of Louis XIV; and maybe the Renaissance classical revival had not happened at all and Shakespeare was merely the final link in a long line of pre-Shakespearian drama.

But the terms pre-Shakespearian, classic revival, and pre-romantic are not good enough to cover the great variety of developments, and art historians have been very helpful in inventing new periods. Most of my teachers at Chicago in the thirties traced the rise of Elizabethan drama from *Gammer Gurton's Needle* and *Gorboduc* to Shakespeare and then had to discuss the decadence of Elizabethan drama of the next four decades. Later, it was a great relief to look at the work of the art historians and borrow the concept of the Baroque age—not a

George R. Kernodle

decadence of Renaissance ideals but turning to new directions; and Wölfflin's *Principles of Art History*, devoted mainly to noting the sharp contrasts in style between Renaissance and Baroque, opened up exciting new ways of studying the spirit of an age in all the arts.

I, for one, have been very grateful to the art historians who have wedged in another period, the Mannerist period (clumsy as the name seemed at first), to separate the Renaissance from the Baroque. The concept of the Mannerist period as a very disturbed transitional period enables us to clarify our concept of Renaissance and Baroque as great achievements in synthesis and order. In a sense, of course, every period is a disturbed and transitional period and every period makes its own attempts to achieve order. I shall suggest several forms of art—the *commedia dell'arte* clowns and Shakespeare's fools, for instance—that seem effective symbols of complex order in the generally disordered Mannerist period. But the concept of the Mannerist period is most helpfully applied, as Wylie Sypher applies it in *Four Stages of Renaissance Style* (New York, 1955), to the plays of Ben Jonson and Shakespeare. If we see the 1590s as a full flowering of the Renaissance, later in England than in Italy, then we can describe the change, far more sudden in England than in Italy, to a period of disillusionment, bitterness and anguish, and call the new period the Mannerist period. Jonson was gay in his bitterness, lashing out at the corruption of the world, while Shakespeare was tortured and anguished in his vision of man as disconnected from old certainties. The Italian painters, Il Rosso and Pontormo, at the beginning of the seventeenth century revolted against the neat form and balance of the Renaissance, and the fifth and sixth books of madrigals of Carlo Gesualdo, published in 1611, show strange new dissonances, unprepared resolutions, and sudden transitions. And we all quote from John Donne's "First Anniversary," expressing his reaction to the new science and philosophy with its vivid phrase "all coherence gone."

In the Sistine Chapel of the Vatican, the two great paintings of Michelangelo dramatize the change from Renaissance to Mannerist. The ceiling is extremely complex, perhaps the most complex painting ever conceived; but it is well organized and controlled. It is articulated by sections, and its architectural features give it a strong structure. It is possible to see contortion and restlessness in some of the human figures, but those figures are subordinated to the overall effect of order and control. Yet at the end of the room is the great Last Judgment painted several decades later by the same painter in a very different mood. In the Last Judgment there is no firm structure at all. There is no architecture except at the top, where disconnected columns fly wildly through the air. The twisted strands of contorted bodies drool down through changing, uncertain space, each part in separate focus, with no sure point of view. The overall impression is one of tortured complexity.

If we make comparisons with the stage, we find major changes in both stage setting and dialogue verse forms that correspond neatly to the differences in style between the Sistine ceiling and the Last Judgment. Both the façade stages of Flanders and London and the perspective stage of Italy are Renaissance architectural structures of separate panels, doorways, and columns, articulated as parts of a unified structure. The show façade was known all over Europe in the street theatres of the Royal Entries by the beginning of the sixteenth century, and was borrowed by the Chambers of Rhetoric in Flanders by the 1530s and by Burbage in London by the 1570s. The Italian perspective setting, with its three-dimensional architectural wings and its painted back shutter, was created about the same time. We know of examples by 1507. It is easy to relate both the façade and the perspective forms to the style and mood of the Renaissance and see how they served for both the royal palaces of tragedy and the street scenes of comedy. When Mannerist drama appears with *Hamlet* and *Lear* in England, we can see how the façade theatre with its open stage could show both Hamlet and Lear, as I suggested in *Shakespeare Survey 12* (1959), as displaced from the façade that was a symbol of the throne and of political order. No new form was necessary. But in Italy the new drama of the end of the sixteenth century demanded a more flexible new form of theatre. Beginning in the 1580s, especially in the new masques and operas, the solid architectural world of the perspective setting dissolved into light, painted, changeable forms. Movable scenery, with flat wings and back shutters, was invented, and between the wings and shutters cloud machines came down, ships moved between rolling waves, and monsters rose from opening rocks or seas. The early architectural settings seem characteristic expressions of the humanist confidence and love of order of the Renaissance, and the settings that changed by magic before the eyes of the spectators seem expressions of the new restlessness and sense of change of the Mannerist age.

It is more difficult to explain the introduction of new forms of dialogue in the same decade—the 1580s—when the theatre of machines was gaining new flexibility, but it is surely no coincidence that in one decade in Italy, France, and England the old stanzaic forms of dialogue were challenged by more flexible forms. In Italy the new form was recitative, which remained the medium for operatic dialogue for several centuries. In F   ~e the new form was the couplet of Alexandrines, which by , two lines in rhyme gave a sense of form without preven! easy flow from one moment to the next. The Alexandrine line of twelve syllables and four accents permits great variety. In England the new form was blank verse, which was even freer than the Alexandrine couplet. In Shakespeare's hands it proved a remarkable adaptable medium that could   mplex, long set speeches and yet easily lead into   r stanzaic forms or prose. Although the new dial   s were used for both static Renaissance clarity and   annerist restlessness, we can see some analogy with the   nges in scenic forms.

But I think there is a far more important idea behind the Mannerist style than the breaking up of the Renaissance synthesis and release of a spirit of restlessness and disorder. The beginning of the seventeenth century saw one of the great crises in the European soul, one of the major changes in Western civilization. Out of that crisis both science and high comedy were born, and the two are very closely related. Science would not have been possible without a major change in patterns of thinking, and the theatre and the other arts had far more to do with the change than has been recognized. Marjorie Nicolson, Victor Harris and others have traced the impact of the new scientific ideas, astronomy most particularly, on literature, and have used Donne's "all coherence gone" as a key phrase. I am convinced that the interrelation is more profound than a sequence of influences. The major change was a separation of man from nature, a change that required not only new philosophical concepts but new ways of feeling. Once they were released by the separation of the objective from the subjective, the new scientists forgot the human in the pursuit of nature. Whitehead traces many of the most difficult problems of the modern world to this bifurcation of the mind. The change might have taken place even if no scientist had seized the possibilities; and surely some kind of high comedy would have appeared after Jonson opened the way. A number of definitions by both philosopher and artist were necessary before the general trend of the age became clear.

The separation of man from nature is defined most vividly in Mannerist tragedy. The four great tragedies of Shakespeare are concerned with the displacement of man from his true position. Lear is deprived of his train of followers and thrust out of doors to huddle with outcasts, to defy the storm, to question the gods, and to put nature itself on trial. Hamlet lurks at the edge while a king sits on the throne which Hamlet should rightfully have. In some of the old legends Hamlet sat in the ashes dressed as a fool. But Shakespeare's Hamlet finds that there is a ursurper fool, Polonius, in charge of the castle. All his intentions are mocked by the actions of others—his love for Ophelia by his mother's corruption, his desire for revenge by Laertes' and Fortinbras' swift revenge of their fathers. Lear gives way to madness and Hamlet survives a little while by playing madness, for madness is the immediate result of displacement—it is indeed the basic displacement. Even in comedy Malvolio was shut up as mad when he forgot his rightful place in the household. Macbeth gained and long held the throne, but he lost his control of reality in a world where fair is foul and foul is fair. He thought he could be objective, but such subjective facts as promises, destiny and ghosts thwarted him. He tried to "cancel the bond" that held him to humanity. Lady Macbeth tried to separate herself from her feminine nature, but when the memory of her father's face and later the memory of blood held her to her nature, she went mad.

While Bacon and Galileo were tentatively exploring the idea of man as an observing animal, watching the world with no feelings, no values, no human response, but only intellectual curiosity, the dramatists were also helping to create a man who only observes, and they found the effort difficult and deeply disturbing. One possibility, of course, is to forget all human values, all myths, dreams, ideas and hopes, and live only in the laboratory or in the applied science shop, controlling as well as

George R. Kernodle

weighing and measuring. That has been the ideal of many in the modern world. In the seventeenth-century world of doubt and conflict, of civil and religious wars, the temptation must have been very strong. Very significant is the anecdote told about Galileo when he was forced by the authorities to recant and deny his scientific discoveries. Walking to the window to look at the stars, he murmured, "Eppur, si muove"—"Just the same, they are moving." The objective world of stars and planets, of atoms and molecules, was welcome because it was free from hatreds, fears and greeds. It was impersonal and without feeling—a solid rock of objective fact in the midst of the surging seas of destructive passion. Ever since Bacon and Galileo there have been men who set out to ... e that rock the entire world and to dry up the ocean of su... /e feeling, of superstitions, fears, myths and delusive far... hat such a drought of feeling could be appalling is pa... e comedy of Molière's *Tartuffe*. Orgon achieves objec... a separation from the subjective turmoil of the world, ... ly from his contact with a religious monster, not a scier... e brags of his new state:

> To keep his precepts is to b ... n,
> And view this dunghill of a . ...d with scorn.
> Yes, thanks to him I'm a changed man indeed.
> Under his tutelage my soul's been freed
> From earthly loves, and every human tie:
> My mother, children, brother and wife could die,
> And I'd not feel a single moment's pain. (I, 282-288)

Cleante comments, "That's a fine sentiment, Brother: most humane."

In *A Midsummer Night's Dream* Shakespeare shows us a scientific man, one who believes only what he can know objectively and is sceptical of imagination and illusion—Theseus, Duke of Athens. But he is such an amiable scientist, willing to indulge young lovers in their deceptive fancies, as he loyally indulges his hempen homespuns in their laughable delusion that they are producing an excellent tragedy. Theseus' famous speech at the beginning of Act V was considered in the nineteenth century and on into my undergraduate days as an excellent definition of poetry—the poet identified with the lunatic and the lover, his eye with a fine frenzy rolling.

And as imagination bodies forth
The forms of things unknown, the poet's pen
Turns them to shapes, and gives to airy nothing
A local habitation and a name. (i,14-17)

The arrogant scientist has always thought that the poet dealt
with things unknown, with airy nothing, and the twentieth
century has suffered as much as the seventeenth over this false
separation of objective from subjective. Only in the last few
decades are we again daring to realize that mathematics and
scientific principles are no more existent in nature than is poetry,
but that mathematics, science, art, comedy and poetry are all
man-made, subjective ways of knowing. And the last few decades, like the early seventeenth century, have found new
comic ways of spanning the subjective and objective, new ways
of knowing a world that may be a place to live in rather than
just a phenomenon to be observed. Theseus puts very neatly the
scientist's distrust of both imagination and human emotion—
both are subject to delusion.

Or in the night, imagining some fear,
How easy is a bush supposed a bear. (V,i,21-22)

Hippolyta answers the scientist with the classic argument of
logic: if several reporters give consistent accounts, the accounts
must have some objective validity.

But Theseus expresses the note of waking after a dream, of
clarity after the delusions of the night. At that moment Shakespeare was willing to accept the complete dichotomy of fact and
fancy, of reality and imagination. A little later he helped to de-
fine one of the great Baroque solutions, a solution that preserved
the imagination by making a metaphysical principle of its lack
of reality—that all existence is illusion, all life a dream. Prospero
implies what Calderón more fully develops, that "la vida es
sueño."

But neither the tragic recognition of displacement nor the
romatic denial of reality in the objective world really offered a
livable solution. The best solution was comedy which spans the
objective and the subjective and off   ment and
participation; and a number   omedy grew out
of the Mannerist a   through Molière to the
superb achiev   ge, Congreve and Sheridan, who

125

raised participation in life to a fine, delightful, if exasperating, game.

In the Mannerist age the most momentous comic achievement took the form of an observing character who stood apart and commented on the action around him—a character who was often too involved and too anguished to show real comic detachment. Part of the time Hamlet stands aside and comments, but there is more objectivity in Marston's Malcontent, who is in disguise, playing the role of one who rails like a licensed fool. In pretending to aid the murderous schemes of those who have stolen his dukedom, the Malcontent anticipates the wise observers of Congreve who lead the dupes on to display fully their foolishness, but there is a vast difference between the grim irony of the Malcontent's revenge and the playful indulgence of Congreve's observers. Jonson's schemers in *The Alchemist* are more complex than Plautus' clever slaves, for the victims deserve their fate, as do even more the victims of Volpone and Mosca. Volpone and Mosca are sometimes more interested in the game than in the booty, wanting to see how far their depraved gulls will go. In *Every Man Out of His Humour*, Jonson sets two observing characters completely outside the action, but they are not impersonal observers; they are stirred and driven by a "Furor Poeticus" to scourge and lash the monstrous deformity of the age, to expose it to public view, to hail it into court and gain a sharp judgment. As one observing character says,

> I will scourge those apes;
> And to these courteous eyes oppose a mirror,
> As large as is the stage whereon we act,
> Where they shall see the time's deformity
> Anatomized in every nerve and sinew.
> With constant courage and contempt of fear. (Induction, 117-122)
> . . . .
> My strict hand
> Was made to seize on vice, and with a gripe,
> Squeeze out the humour of such spongy notices
> As lick up every idle vanity. (Induction, 143-146)

Shakespeare was not to be outdone by Jonson in bitter observing characters. In *Troilus and Cressida* he creates one for each of his main themes—Pandarus to comment on lechery, and

Thersites on war—"wars and lechery." In this play nearly all the scenes have observers, sometimes observers watching the observers. Certainly Shakespeare is dramatizing man's detachment, but not really his comic detachment. The play is far from a delightful comedy; we would rather call it a Mannerist, disillusioned echo of the gorgeous Renaissance love poem *Romeo and Juliet*. Romeo's bright suns and heavenly angels are replaced by Troilus' bawdy crows.

The railing character is put in a more genial context in *As You Like It*. Jaques is fascinated by fools and wants to crow like Chanticleer that fools should be so deep contemplative. He wants the liberty of the fool to attack the world.

> Give me leave
> To speak my mind, and I will through and through
> Cleanse the foul body of th' infected world. (II,vii,58-60)

But the Duke reproves him for wanting to disgorge the sins he had caught in living too much in the world. At the end he refuses to join in the festivities.

It is the court fools, the professional jesters of Shakespeare, who achieve the balance between living in the world and watching it from a distance. They see the coarseness and stupidity of the world without turning away in disgust. They skirt the abyss of madness and see its dangers, but they do not fall in. They have had full experience but, unlike Jaques, they are not saddened. As Rosalind says, "I had rather have a fool to make me merry than experience to make me sad."

Touchstone is completely disillusioned, detached from the world, but not for a second does he attack what he is observing. He pokes fun at the bows and hat-doffing manners of the court, he mimics Orlando's lovesick poems and Silvius' plaints for Phebe; he mocks the Duke's sermons and Jaques' moralizing. He punctures every illusion of those around him. His wooing and wedding of Audrey is a triumphant combination of satire and participation. He achieves the first Baroque resolution, the theatrical resolution: he is spectator and actor at the same time. He sees his own limitations as he sees those of others and yet merrily accepts life with all its limitations. What modern hero of an existentialist play ever faced so completely the loss of all glamorous illusion as to say of his bride, "Well, praised be the gods for thy foulness. Sluttishness may come hereafter"? Or who could be more cheerfully adjusted than this bridegroom introducing with pride "a poor virgin, sir, an ill-favoured thing, sir, but mine own"?

More than Touchstone, Feste is set apart as an observer, but he is also a ring-leader of the festival revels. Shakespeare apparently had once intended to have him take part in showing up the deluded steward Malvolio, but changed his mind and split the role to let a frolicking servant, Fabian, join Sir Toby and Sir Andrew in gulling Malvolio. Feste is left to touch on all groups, teasing or observing them but involved with none. At the Stratford, Ontario, Festival in 1957, Tyrone Guthrie directed Feste as a gray, bitter old man, tortured by a sense of pain into torturing others; but he is usually played as a light-hearted sprite who sees through the delusions of others and knows that clear-headed playing of the game is the one way of avoiding madness. The third time I directed the play it suddenly occurred to me that Feste recognizes that Viola is a girl in disguise. Then the scene at the beginning of the third act takes on new life, with Feste calling her "Sir" fifteen times in a few speeches and teasing money from her. She is grateful that he will not interfere with her game. At the end the fool must look after the drunkard, Sir Toby, and deliver the madman, Malvolio.

In *King Lear* the fool cannot deliver the madman; he can only lead him lovingly into madness, making sure that he sees clearly his own foolish predicament. He can stay with Lear and teach him the tragic and Christian paradox that he who loses his life may gain it. "I will tarry, the fool will stay, and let the wise man fly."

At about the same time as Shakespeare and his poet-singer-actor Robert Armin created these three fools, the *commedia dell' arte* reached its peak, not with one motley jester in a courtly world but with a whole company of clowns, all fantastically costumed and all but the young lovers in masks—a timeless image of the duality of appearance and reality. Not only were their main costumes very different from the street clothes of the time, but they were constantly disguising—as magicians, as ghosts, as each other—and constantly interrupting each other. All was appearance, disguise, change. Here was not only an image of Mannerist displacement but a comic solution. The solution was not a sad acceptance of illusion, as in *The Tempest* or *Life Is a Dream*, but an acceptance of complexity and bafflement for the fun of it. One element of acceptance was the sheer virtuosity of the performance. The seventeenth century worshipped the skilled performer, the virtuoso tenor or castrato-soprano, the king who could dominate an assembly or a parade or a tournament, the priest who could conduct a spectacular ceremony. And the most amazing virtuoso was the *commedia* actor, who could leap through windows, box an ear with his foot, sing a song and adapt the words as he went along, burst into the most eloquent yet absurd impromptu speeches. Laughter was a far more successful, if more difficult, resolution of the tensions of the age than spectacular opera or operatic pageantry of church and king.

The *commedia* was a big step toward the achievement of full high comedy. It gave each character his chance in turn. It was a Ballet of controlled interactions among equals. Yet it was essentially an interaction of attack and interruption, of alternate triumph and pain. In a similar spirit, the scene of Portia and Nerissa triumphing over their spouses about the rings has some of the balance and precise light step of a ballet and the thrust and parry of a fencing match. The scene is set in moonlight, with talk about harmonious music and the harmony of the spheres, and we know that the discord is only a suspended resolution, but it is a game only for the women: for the men it is pain. The scene is only a more charming, half-musical version of the Plautine farce of error; it has gone only halfway to high comedy.

There are similar musical balances in *As You Like It*, but the men again are at a disadvantage. It is not their game. In directing the play several years ago I discovered that it is easy to indicate that Orlando knows that Ganymede is a woman and is surely the same princess he has recently fallen in love with. He is fascinated and puzzled. What will she do next? Every time he comes close to her, ready to speak directly, she puts him off with another play of wit. He can only hint that it is not a very satisfying game for him and wait until her moment of disclosure. It is a game, but not quite a game between equals.

In Molière's plays the ancient game of deception makes all characters equal. The master who tries to beat the truth out of his servant gets only a lie. The father who tries to force his children finds that they have tricked him. The husband who distrusts his wife finds that he has provoked her to deceive him.

George R. Kernodle

Molière is especially interested in the bafflement of the character who tries to use his power to force human relations and
finds that he is totally helpless. His only chance to win over his
servant, his child, or his wife is absolute trust and respect. A
half-century before Locke and a century before Jefferson,
Molière is defining the absolute independence and equality of
individuals. But complete sceptic that he was, Molière shows
more often the failures than the few times a character learns to
play a more mature role of self-knowledge and love.

The best game between equals is the game of wit, and in
several plays Shakespeare is fascinated by wit combats. Beatrice and Benedict court each other with verbal sparring as truly
as Petruchio courts Katherine with his strong arm and a whip.
Wit is courtship also in *Love's Labour's Lost*. But wit is attack
and separation, bound up with the idea of scorn, cutting and
stabbing. Benedict says, "She speaks poniards and every word
stabs." Wit establishes the lovers as separate and equal, but it
cannot bring them together. In Shakespeare, as in Restoration
comedy, wit is particularly associated with pride, but in Shakespeare pride keeps the lovers apart. Only when Beatrice and
Benedict relinquish pride do they admit love, and only when
they are threatened with grave danger do they drop the game
of conflict. In the same way, Laurey and Curly in *Green Grow
the Lilacs* and its musical form *Oklahoma!* have taken stances of
sexual battle that they cannot escape until danger in the minor
plot makes them give up their independence. In Molière's *The
Misanthrope*, Alceste and Célimène reach an impasse of pride
and separate forever. It is the high achievement of Etherege and
Congreve that their proud couples do come together and still
keep their pride and independence. Mirabell in *The Way of the
World* thinks it is important for his wife to get her fortune, not
from greed but so that she may keep her independence. Sir
Peter Teazle in *The School for Scandal* finds that his wife's
dependence on him for her expenses is the source of most of
their vexation and that she will be much easier to live with when
he settles money on her in her own name. Like Mirabell, Sir
Peter likes Lady Teazle better for being proud and independent. He enjoys their differences, and after their second-act
quarrel he says,

So—I have gained much by my intended expostulation! Yet with what a charming air she contradicts everything I say, and how pleasantly she shows her contempt for my authority! Well, though I can't make her love me, there is great satisfaction in quarrelling with her; and I think she never appears to such advantage as when she is doing everything in her power to plague me. (II,i,112-118)

In spite of their difference in age, or because they admit their differences, they are very fond of each other and make a good couple.

The pert rural girl who has had no freedom at home becomes Lady Teazle and blossoms into one of the fashionable ladies of the town, with great respect for the freedom of society. When Sir Peter condemns the gossip sessions, she proudly defends society: "What, would you restrain the freedom of speech?" When he condemns her for joining the gossips, she defines society as a good-humoured meetings of equals:

Why, I believe I do bear a part with a tolerable grace. But I vow I bear no malice against the people I abuse: when I say an ill-natured thing, 'tis out of pure good humour; and I take it for granted they deal exactly in same manner with me. (II,i,102-106)

Sheridan makes distinctions in kinds of scandal, from dangerous lies to indiscreet guesses. But it is very clear that when Sir Peter wants to hide something about his own family he is inviting the silly gossips to make guesses. He has only to show the truth and the danger of scandal is over. But he is afraid of being laughed at. The final painful achievement of Sir Peter is to laugh at himself. He is right to drive out of his house the leering, taunting fools, but his good friends also laugh at him and he cannot drive them out. He is part of society, and society has the right to comment on human behaviour. In learning how wrong he had been about Joseph he is humbled and sees that a general disillusion can be healthy. "Sir Oliver," he says, "we live in a damned wicked world, and the fewer we praise the better."

A number of plays and movies of the past decade show signs of a new period of high comedy, and it too is born out of a crisis in man's definition of reality, another change in the concepts of objective and subjective. At the beginning of the twentieth century, naturalism was beginning to dominate the main fields of art, and positivism seemed triumphant in philosophy.

Strindberg alternated between anguished naturalistic plays and tortured dream sonatas, finding no stable place in either fact or fancy. Pirandello made his version of the old idea that life is illusion but found no such calm confidence as Prospero found. To Pirandello the illusions were multiple, but all real and none of them in the control of the observer. Illusion meant delusion, pain or insanity. O'Neill picked up from Ibsen and Nietzsche the idea that a life-lie is necessary even if it is impossible to sustain and is totally unrelated to reality. Here was the same restless scepticism that we see in the earlier Mannerist age. The achievements in science and technology in the nineteenth and early twentieth century were impressive, and for many minds they promised liberation from hard work, from provincial limitations, and above all from old hatreds, fears and superstitions. But the promises were as illusory as the sixteenth-century humanist promise of a synthesis of classical and Christian philosophy. The rise of totalitarian governments, the two world wars, the atomic bomb, the endless cold war, and above all the loss of personal identity in the lonely crowd, have brought a major new disillusionment. Something was wrong with a definition of objectivity without subjective values, a definition that made man himself a thing. It is not surprising that many people turned to the more extreme forms of existentialism to reaffirm the absolute validity of the subjective. If science and history are created without regard to human values, then science and history are literally valueless. The theatre of the absurd, with its repudiation of all traditional order, was an expression of protest and rebellion.

Actually many scientists themselves have radically changed their concepts of objectivity. Physicists have had to live with two inconsistent theories of light radiation, the quantum and the wave theory—a situation almost as disturbing as the sixteenth- and seventeenth-century multiplicity of suns, planets, religions and continents. Now physicists recognize that what they observe is partly determined by what instruments they use and what theories they start with, and on the other hand that the models they make are not exact representations of objective reality but subjective organizations of some aspects of reality. The scientists themselves are trying to span the separation of subjective and objective by including the observer as well as the phenomenon observed.

Again in comedy there are signs of new definitions of comic detachment similar to those in the old Mannerist age. For instance, the observing character again offers a way of being both actor and watcher, and his presence suggests a new kind of high comedy. Two films—*La Dolce Vita* and *Blow-up*—show the painful attemps of a reporter in the one and a photographer in the other to take part in the chaotic world they are recording and find some meaningful relationship. The play *Marat/Sade* is almost completely mad, and the two leading characters offer such diametrically opposed political theories that there seems no way of reconciling them. Yet we think that the French Revolution did accomplish something, or, to put it another way, that the people who survived it did eventually rescue some values and manage to solve some of the political dilemmas. To see the movie version is to realize how much a comedy *Marat/Sade* is. As the camera concentrates on faces, one or two at a time, there is too much identification with the pain and insanity. We laugh much more easily when we see people in their social contexts. In spite of the extreme subjectivism of the existentialists we do accept the idea of man in society, no matter how insane the society may seem.

I can remember in the 1920s and 1930s how smugly we condemned the Elizabethans for laughing at insanity on the stage. We thought we could not be so coarse or cruel. Yet now we are cultivating a theatre of cruelty and are fascinated by half-comic madness on the stage. Three years ago I saw in Rome a stunning production of Middleton and Rowley's *The Changeling* with the chorus of lunatics kept on the stage throughout the play. Where *Marat/Sade* studied politics against a background of insanity, *I Lunatici* studied personal-psychological relations as surrounded by and emerging from insanity. The play seemed both Elizabethan and very modern. Let us hope that we are emerging into at least a laughing insanity.

Some of the early one-act plays of Edward Albee are absurd or satiric and produce laughter only when the audience is completely detached from sympathy. But several of his long plays approach high comedy. In London Kenneth Tynan scolded the actors and the audience for laughter at *Who's Afraid of Virginia Woolf?* He did not want to recognize that the play is in some respects a high comedy. The movie version, played partly in moonlight and isolating single characters in close-ups, caused less laughter than the stage version. But on stage the game of attack and parry played in a small living room was comic. It is a bitter and painful game but one that leads both couples to self-knowledge and to an understanding and acceptance of each other.

The Lion in Winter is another study of independence and conflict, as Henry II and his queen, Eleanor of Aquitaine, realize that their conflict is greater than their love. Their own lives are too caught up in the web of historical forces for an easy solution of their personal feelings. The ending is not a happy reconciliation, as in Congreve or Sheridan, nor yet a final hopeless separation as in *The Misanthrope*. The Christmas reunion over, Eleanor sadly returns to her prison, with more understanding of her difficult husband and of herself, knowing that Easter will come with another chance to continue their complex relationship.

There is grim comic irony in the painful bewilderment of the two principals in *Rosencrantz and Guildenstern Are Dead*, but the troupe of Players have a creative control of their world that sets them ahead of the two principals and moves the play nearer to high comedy than its model, *Waiting for Godot*. By playing death in all its forms, the Players have lost their fear of it and, as creative artists, able to make both a drama and a game of their lives, they find some meaning in existence. Cheerfully disillusioned already, they do not demand as much of life as Rosencrantz and Guildenstern, and they find far more.

When we realize how long it was from the bitter comedy of Ben Jonson to the more urbane disillusionment of Molière and to the brisk, witty players of games in Congreve and Sheridan, we can hope that our Mannerist age of confusion, disillusion and pain has made a start towards a new high comedy—a new way of watching the world and also being a part of it. "For what do we live," says Jane Austen's Mr. Bennet, "but to make sport for our neighbours, and laugh at them in our turn?"

Continuity and Innovation
in Shakespeare*

JOHN LAWLOR

I want to put before you some thoughts on Shakespeare's theatrecraft, those skills and resources which are characteristic of Shakespeare the working dramatist. What is central to the thoughts I have to offer is what has been foremost in the conference's proceedings—an awareness that it is to the theatre that all interpretation must consistently be referred if we are not to risk dealing in unrealities.

I first thought of organizing these remarks around a theme which has interested me for some time—the continuity of Shakespeare's creative imagination and the innovations we see from time to time in his art,[1]—but I recalled Housman's astringent observation that a scholar confronted by alternatives "cannot but feel in every fibre of his being that he is a donkey between two bundles of hay." Worse, the poor man is likely to suppose that "if one bundle of hay is removed he will cease to be a donkey."[2] Well, there is a kind of comfort in this. Unlike the textual scholar, I am under no obligation to choose one alternative and to reject the other—to affirm continuity in Shakespeare's art at the expense of innovation, or vice versa. That has often enough been done, and its influence is still strong, if latent. On the contrary, in any argument of that kind one would wish to hold steadily to both notions. If what is

---

*This paper was given as an after-dinner talk on the last evening of the conference.

[1] See my "Continuity and Innovation in Shakespeare's Dramatic Career," REL, V (1964), 11-23.

[2] A. E. Housman, Selected Prose, ed. John Carter (Cambridge, 1961), p. 35.

relatively constant in Shakespeare can be shown, then the innovations, the points at which significant departure is made,
will be strikingly evident. But I thought it best to steer away
from alternatives altogether and rather to ask simply the hard
but inevitable question. "What is the veritably Shakespearian?" How can we hope to get, consistently, at that which is
central in each play?

I

Jan Kott's pursuit of Shakespeare as "Our Contemporary"
has often enough been discussed since the appearance of his
book in 1966. Perhaps the fairest way of regarding this whole
proposition is to say that if, as some would hold, it is an evil
(a mere projection of the present upon the past), then it is surely
a necessary evil. Those who are confident that they can place
Shakespeare in a wholly authentic Elizabethan–Jacobean past
are deceiving themselves. The briefest words of commentary,
the simplest placing of an actor on whatever form of stage,
even a mediumistic mode of reverential silence, are all condition-
ed by the present from within which the exponent—scholar,
producer, or both in one—looks out upon his author. We must
accommodate or close the subject. "Unaccommodated" Shakespeare—a Shakespeare safely insulated from our own concerns
and predispositions—is an impossibility. I must only add that
we touch the fringe of that impossibility in a Shakespeare who
is adapted to teaching schoolboys and undergraduates spelling,
mythology, historical allusions, and the like; and that we have
not always done better when we have gone on to more elaborate
inferences from the body of his work. There are many ways of
immunizing a major author; and societies have ordinarily done
so in the interests of "education." But that makes it all the more
necessary that we know what has been done when an author
has been made the staple of courses. Actor, producer and
audience alike come to the play with their minds in some sort
already made up. To unmake them drastically, by presenting
a pretendedly authentic version, may be one salutary way of
re-awakening attention, but it cannot claim any specially
privileged status.

The attempt to remove Shakespeare from contamination by
latter-day readers and audiences (editors, too, one must add),

can take another form. Instead of pressing for an 'historical" understanding—Shakespeare in a fully Elizabethan–Jacobean setting, from the large generalities of world-picture down to the detail of playhouse structure—critics have sometimes asked us to envisage a timeless Shakespeare, one whose grandeurs and miseries are those of all humanity. I do not, of course, wish to deny that there is a sense, and a most valuable sense, in which a major artist can speak unforcedly to people of widely differing races and beliefs and, equally, to those of markedly divergent mores within a single tradition. This, surely, is one of the things we mean when we speak of a major artist. But these "timeless" views are subject to two grave shortcomings. If we can bring ourselves to examine the universal chorus of praise, we find there is no clear ground of agreement upon particulars. To paraphrase Sir Thomas Browne, it is easiest to be lost in an *O altitudo*! Secondly, the timelessness claimed is itself the product of a particular time—the notion peculiarly dear to nineteenth-century romanticism that the deepest personality of the artist lies within his work and, in consequence, that the task of criticism is to seek most diligently for that personality. Dowden's equation of the Shakespearian life with the Shakespearian canon needs no more refutation than the late C. J. Sisson's "The Mythical Sorrows of Shakespeare."[3] But are we yet wholly free of this kind of preconception? When Philip Edwards, introducing a valuable survey of the last plays, begins by characterizing "the control and concentration" evident in the great tragedies,[4] then it may be that an acceptable description will lodge itself with the reader as pejorative criticism. "Control and concentration" should be so self-evidently good! We need to hold steadily before our minds the characteristic limitations as well as the undeniable virtues of control and concentration, if we are to approach the last plays without the preconception that they are a decline, a diminution in creative power, from the peak achievement of the Bradleian big four. To complement older assumptions we need to murmur the maxims of our own age, of which the most penetrating, surely, is D. H. Lawrence's dictum: "Never trust the artist. Trust the

---

[3] British Academy Shakespeare Lecture (1934).
[4] "Shakespeare's Romances: 1900-1957," *Shakespeare Survey II* (1958), 1-18. (Professor Edwards himself concludes by suggesting valid approaches to these plays in their own right, pleading in particular for recognition of the "delight" of romance as constituting its distinctive "catharsis.")

tale."[5] It is put with a different emphasis by T. S. Eliot: "The more perfect the artist, the more completely separate in him will be the man who suffers and the mind which creates."[6] On this view, if the writer is not the patient of his work, recognizing and submitting to the developing necessities of that work as it grows into organic unity, then he is not likely to summon any continuing interest. Equally, if criticism obstinately projects upon the work its own preconceptions, including images of the writer himself, then the work must remain finally opaque —fortifying, it may be, the self-esteem of a variety of critics and underpinning educational systems, but abstract and infertile because immovably external. Either way, our notion of what it is that we are dealing with, the grain and joint of the Shakespearian *oeuvre*, is fatally overlaid.

II

Housman's donkey of an editor may have come back to your minds. If the creature is not to choose between the alternatives of present and past—the bale labelled "Shakespeare our Contemporary" and that marked variously "Shakespeare the Elizabethan," "Shakespeare the Timeless One"—what shall he do? E. E. Kellett once spoke of the whirligig of taste; is the critic's part merely to wait until it brings in its appropriate revenges? Perhaps we should echo Claudio, caught between alternative hypotheses, crying that these are matters "I stagger in." Well, there are considerations which will help us stagger as little as possible.

First, we must at every stage remind ourselves of the width of Shakespeare's production. For example, if we recall the variety of the plays listed as tragedies in the Folio, we shall be best placed to assess the true relation of control and concentration to Shakespeare's whole tragic range. In that light we may well agree with Kenneth Muir that "There is no such thing as Shakespearean Tragedy: there are only Shakespearean tragedies."[7] This, whether in comedy or tragedy, is the only

---

[5] *Studies in Classic American Literature*, Phoenix edition (London, 1964), p. 2.
[6] "Tradition and the Individual Talent," *Selected Essays* (London, 1932), p. 18.
[7] "Shakespeare and the Tragic Pattern," *Proceedings of the British Academy 1958* (London, 1959), p. 146.

profitable approach; otherwise, we shall find ourselves arguing in the tight circle of our own predispositions. Certain plays
will have been selected to illustrate the genre—because they
are the ones that do illustrate it. The same consideration must
apply to any other categorization within Shakespeare's total
production—not only in terms of which plays are to be included
in any one grouping, but, before all else, a readiness to test the
categorization-label itself. For example, any treatment of
"problem comedies" must take due notice of the extent to
which "problems" in the sense intended are present and active
in the comedies as a whole.

This leads to my second consideration. An unprejudiced
attention to any one grouping in its full extent must direct
attention to common features among plays not obviously alike.
I have suggested elsewhere[8] that if we do take into account all
Shakespeare's tragedies when we are trying to formulate notions of what constitutes the tragic, then our survey cannot
easily exclude either *Romeo and Juliet* (as an early work too
little concerned with effective characterization) or *Antony
and Cleopatra* (regarded as a falling off from the sustained
"connective" work of the Bradleian big four). Both these plays
have striking endings—last acts in which union between the
lovers transcends all other considerations. These truly theatrical endings—if we can rid the word theatrical of all pejorative association—may lead us to look again at the structure of
other tragedies. For example, Lear's reunion with Cordelia
(IV.vii) is the unforgettable turning-point, a restoration of
unlooked-for happiness, that reverses the mutual disclaimers
of the play's first scene and sustains Lear's eventual acceptance
of the blessedness of a walled prison. Then, isolation with Cordelia can be embraced joyfully—"We two alone will sing like
birds i' th' cage" (V.iii.9)—and the rite of mutual forgiveness is
to be endlessly re-enacted, as a kind of sanctified game:

When thou dost ask me blessing, I'll kneel down
And ask of thee forgiveness. (V.iii.10-11)

How is the great turning-point prepared for? I do not mean in
a narrowly thematic or plot-structural sense. We can all see

[8] "Romeo and Juliet," in *Early Shakespeare*, ed. John Russell Brown and Bernard
Harris, Stratford-upon-Avon Studies 3 (London, 1961), 123-43.

the logic of events that has led to this point and we can feel the blessed paradox of the reversal of Lear's expectation,

> Pray, do not mock me
> I am a very foolish, fond old man. (IV.vii.59-60)

Much more, how does Shakespeare prepare us, the audience, for the emotional fulfilment-as-reversal that takes place here? I believe that if we concentrate on the gesture that is central to this scene we have the most revealing clue. Lear kneels to his daughter; and he is raised by her: "No, Sir, *you* must not kneel" (IV.vii.59). The King and father has knelt to the subject and child, and in this willing subordination the new order established by Lear—a world turned upside-down—is reinverted, turned the right way up. What Lear in the first confusion of his senses takes to be the manifestation of a higher power than his own ("Thou art a soul in bliss") is indeed so, but in entirely human terms.

King Lear then kneels; so did Leir in the old play, *King Leir*. But there, as Kenneth Muir observes, "the scene topples over into absurdity,"[9] with repeated kneelings and risings. Shakespeare has sharpened his moment of crisis to one kneeling, one great reversal; but if we look into the fabric of the play we shall find that there is another kneeling of father to daughter, in Act II, Scene iv. At that point Lear kneels in savage mimicry of himself as petitioner:

> Do you but mark how this becomes the house:
> 'Dear daughter, I confess that I am old'. (II.iv,151-2)

Regan's reply is coldly appropriate to this pantomime: "Good sir, no more; these are unsightly tricks" (II.iv.155). The play goes forward with renewed impetus, but the significant action lies in the web of the spectator's cumulative attention to the play. At the right time it is re-engaged, to sustain the authority of a single and crucial kneeling, when Lear does gladly what he had once mimed in brutal contempt.

My third point, then, makes itself. Clearly, we need to learn what Rudolf Stamm has to teach us about "theatrical physiognomy," the skill of searching the text for all indications it can

---

[9] *King Lear*, New Arden edition (London, 1952), p. xxx.

give us of the play in performance;[10] but the special approach I am suggesting is that we should scrutinize all instances within any one play of the business of definitive gesture that invests a major scene; and we should look for a preluding, often with burlesque or ironic overtones, of that action which is to be serious and fully decisive at the turning-point. Such a study, of course, is widely applicable. I have dealt with kneeling in *King Lear*. There is a moment of intensity in *II Henry IV* where the former Hal, now the monarch, summons the Lord Chief Justice. The Lord Chief Justice, expecting sentence, submits to his sovereign:

> After this cold considerance, sentence me;
> And, as you are a King, speak in your state
> What I have done that misbecame my place. (V.ii.98-100)

He kneels. But expectation is reversed; the Lord Chief Justice is raised by Hal:

> There is my hand ...
> ....
> And I will stoop and humble my intents
> To your well-practis'd wise directions. (V.ii.117, 120-1)

Justice is placed at the right hand of monarchy; the stage action moves from the posture of submission to the position of authority. If we look for the preluding of this movement earlier in the two parts of *Henry IV*, we find it, I believe, in two places, as yet unfocused in the swirl of events: first, in the play-acting at Eastcheap (*I Henry IV*, II.iv) where there is both a mock-obeisance, as Hal defers to Falstaff-as-King ("here is my leg"), and also an up-and-down movement from the "throne," as Falstaff, the would-be authority, is "deposed" by an impatient claimant:

> Dost thou speak like a King? Do thou stand for me, and I'll play my father. (II.iv.418-9)

---

[10] See in particular his article, "Elizabethan Stage-practice and the transmutation of source-material by the Dramatists," *Shakespeare Survey 12* (1959), 64-70, and the two collections of essays informed by the same approach: *Zwischen Vision und Wirklichkeit* (Bern, 1964); *The Shaping Powers at Work* (Heidelberg, 1967).

The mock-courtesies of this scene, and the mimic professions of certainty, are counterpointed by the scene between father and son (*II Henry IV*, IV.v.) when the son must kneel to make his solemn avowal:

> If I affect it more
> Than as your honour and as your renown,
> Let me no more from this obedience rise,
> Which my most inward, true, and duteous spirit
> Teacheth this prostrate and exterior bending. (IV.v.145-9)

Now Hal can be raised by his father and treated as a counsellor:

> Come hither, Harry, sit thou by my bed,
> And hear, I think, the very latest counsel
> That ever I shall breathe. (IV.v.182-4)

What Henry V at the outset of his reign does for a suppliant Lord Chief Justice is a re-enactment of what he had last received from his dying father; and the gesture seals at once not only the ascendancy of Law but also the approval of a true surrogate-father ("You shall be as a father to my youth"). It is in these ways that Shakespearian drama sustains a current of demonstrative energy, a pattern of action that draws upon the deepest yet most ordinary sense of what we may properly call "ritual," the means by which human beings assure themselves as well as others of their deepest intents. Recognition of this, and its effective re-enactment upon the stage, must prevent Shakespeare's work from ever being mistaken for merely a drama of ideas.

With this understanding I come to my fourth point. One of the more serviceable critical instruments we can employ is the tension—if that is the right word; I mean a fruitful interplay in the dramatist's working imagination—between (adopting Bacon's terms) "poesy" and "history."[11] The creative artist must select and shape, and some notion of the moral status, the acceptability or unacceptability of particular predispositions, intentions, and acts on the part of the persons of the play must inevitably come through, heightened or qualified as necessary by choric

---

[11] *The Advancement of Learning*, ed. Thomas Case, World's Classics edition (London, 1906; rpt. 1960), II.iv.1,2, pp. 96-97.

utterances, confidant-type commentary, or set-piece declaration. That is the "poesy," the necessary condition on which we have art at all. But Shakespeare, it has been readily seen in all epochs, draws upon a "fund of Nature." There is (as some earlier critics noted with disapproval) no obvious moral of a copybook kind; comic and tragic effects are mixed; "even," as Johnson noticed, "where the agency is supernatural the dialogue is level with life"—a phrase that takes in the widest implications of Shakespeare's art. What is central in Shakespeare—and, as R. W. Chambers long ago noticed,[12] is continuous in him—is the sense that ruthless individualism (the world of "I am I") *can* attain its objectives; but in attaining them it must know itself dispossessed of human status, cut off from all natural feeling. Macbeth's recognition that "honour, love, obedience, troops of friends" (V.iii.25), he "must not look to have," speaks for all wilful transgressors. In this sense history in Bacon's meaning is faithfully adhered to: here is a drama which puts before us in unmistakable, because veritably human, terms "the successes and issues of actions not so agreeable to the merits of virtue and vice." But if the greatest disaster is achieved in isolation, then transcendent happiness is to be found in union— alike between parent and child, and between man and woman in the bond of love, from *Romeo and Juliet* to *Antony and Cleopatra* in the sequence of tragedies, and so to the last plays where the lost are found, the dead brought back to life, and children lead their parents to an unlooked-for happiness. The striking thing is that Shakespeare's moments of greatest theatre, where one might expect art or poesy to be at its height, are in fact triumphant assertions of nature or history—the limitless capacity of human nature to accept and, in the accepting, to restore happiness. I would like to see us following up the late D. G. James's perceptive handling of poesy and history[13]—but in terms not primarily of content (theme and "values") but of gesture, tempo and business, the distinctive lineaments of the play in performance which we may discern in the plain text before us.

---

[12] See "The Jacobean Shakespeare and *Measure for Measure*," British Academy Shakespeare Lecture (1937), expanded in *Man's Unconquerable Mind* (London, 1939), pp. 250-310.
[13] *The Dream of Learning* (Oxford, 1951).

This is, I believe, the chief safeguard against our tendency, most often involuntary, to galvanize the Shakespearian play into life. It is natural that we should try to do that, and it is in a sense creditable, as a reaction against the mere torpor of treating Shakespeare as a Great Author, to be studied, analysed and finally held apart from life as we encounter it. Honest examination of the play in performance will be some safeguard against that, for its first step is to find "every blur a challenge,"[14] and so to move away from mere impatience with what is at first opaque or elusive. We may, of course, find in any one instance that the means of communicating something distinctively Elizabethan to a modern audience are far from easy; and questions of the overall balance to be attempted for a modern audience will necessarily arise. Every good director must have the courage to cut his losses, and judgments will differ on what can be centrally upheld and what must be understated or only marginally shown. But to do these things we must first grasp what is central to the play in its own right. Only then can we estimate how far the Shakespeare we perform can become the audience's contemporary. We shall run endless risks, not so much of theatrical failure as of mere misdirection of effort, if we ever lose sight of the fact that our task is not so much to interpret Shakespeare as to let Shakespeare interpret us—to bring it about that we are contemporaries of Shakespeare's as well as his being our contemporary.

[14] *Fourteenth Century Verse and Prose*, ed. Kenneth Sisam (Oxford, 1921), p. xliii.

The Contributors

HERBERT BERRY, Professor of English, University of Saskatchewan. Author of articles on the Elizabethan theatre.

W. REAVLEY GAIR, Associate Professor of English, University of New Brunswick. Author of articles on Renaissance Literature.

GEORGE R. KERNODLE, Professor of Dramatic Arts, University of Arkansas. Author of *From Art to Theatre* and other books, and articles on theatrical history.

T. J. KING, Associate Professor of English, City College of the City University of New York. Author of *Shakespearean Staging, 1599-1642* and articles on the Elizabethan theatre.

J. A. LAVIN, Professor of English, University of British Columbia. Editor of several Elizabethan plays and author of articles on sixteenth and seventeenth century bibliography.

JOHN LAWLOR, Professor of English Language and Literature, University of Keele. Author of *The Tragic Sense in Shakespeare* and of many articles on the Elizabethan drama.

CLIFFORD LEECH, Professor of English, University College, Toronto. Until recently, General Editor of the *Revels Plays,* and author of numerous books and articles on the Elizabethan drama.

GLYNNE WICKHAM, Professor of Drama and Head of the Drama Department, University of Bristol. Author of *Early English Stages, 1300-1660* (2 vols.) and of many articles on theatrical history.

Index

146

Index

126; *Bartholomew Fair*, 25, 31; *Catiline*, 99; *Eastward Ho*, 15-31; *Every Man in His Humour* (prologue), 11; *Every Man Out of His Humour*, 126; *Isle Of Dogs*, 85; "Masque at Barriers," 92; *Masque of Blackness*, 99; *Masque of Oberon*, 92; *Poetaster*, 24; *Sejanus* (prefatory epistle), 7; *Volpone*, 23, 126
Jordan, Israel, 39

King Leir, 140
Knight of Malta, The, 11
Kott, Jan, 136
Kyd, Thomas: *The Spanish Tragedy*, 19, 25

Langley, Francis, 34, 38-39, 40
Langley, Richard, 39
Lawrence, D. H., 137
Leake, John, 43
Leech, Clifford: ed. *Two Noble Kinsmen*, 69; "The Dramatist's Independence," 69
Leigh, Sir James, 17, 107, 109
Leyland, John, 101-2
Lion in Winter, The, 134
Lover's Melancholy (John Ford), 74
Love's Cruelty (James Shirley), 4

Mannerism, 119-34
Maps of London: Agas, 35; Horwood, 43; Ogilby and Morgan, 43-59 *passim*, 60-65; Ordnance Survey 1875, 57, 60, 65; 1848-1850, 60, 65; 1894-1896, 57, 65; 1969, 65; Rocque, 56
Marat/Sade, 133
Marlowe, Christopher: *Tamburlaine*, 25; *Edward II*, 73
Marmion, Shackerly: *The Antiquary*, 100, 115-18; *Holland's Leaguer*, 117
Marston, John: *Eastward Ho*, 15-31; *Malcontent, The*, 14, 73, 126; *Satiromastix*, 17, 73
Massinger, Philip: *The City Madam*, 4
Matthew of Westminster: *Flores historiarum*, 103
Mauncey, James, 94
Mead, Joseph, 113

Messalina (Nathanael Richards); title page, 3, 4
Michelangelo: Sistine Chapel, 120
Middleton, Thomas, 17; *Changeling, The*, 133; *Friar Bacon*, 73; *A Game at Chess*, 85, 87; *Honest Whore, The*, 17; *More Dissemblers Besides Women*, 31
Milton, John: *Comus*, 99
Molière, 125, 129; *Misanthrope, The*, 130, 134; *Tartuffe*, 124
Muir, Kenneth, 138, 140
Munday, Anthony, 96, 97; *London's Love for Prince Henry*, 92; *Triumphs of re-united Britania*, 87, 89-91

Nashe, Thomas: *Pierce Pennilesse*, 106
Needler, John, 50
Needler, Thomas, 42-60 *passim*
Nevile, Sir Henry, 108
Nicoll, Allardyce: on *The Widow's Tears*, 31
Nicolson, Marjorie, 122
Nietzsche, F. W., 132

O'Neill, Eugene, 132

Paris, Matthew: *Historia maior*, 103
Parker, Matthew, 101-15 *passim; De Antiquitate Britanicae Ecclesiae*, 104
Parrott, Thomas Marc: on *Eastward Ho*, 27; on *Eastward Ho* and *Westward Ho*, 20
Partridge, Eric: on *Eastward Ho*, 27
Pirandello, Luigi, 132
Poley, Edmund and family, 34-59 *passim*
Pontormo, 120
Prouty, C. T.: on Trinity Hall, 2-3

Revenger's Tragedy, The (Tourneur, Cyril), 19
Rice, John, 92
Roscarrock, Nicholas, 107
Rosencrantz and Guildenstern Are Dead (T. Stoppard), 134
Rowan, D. F.: Jones/Webb Theatre project, 2n
Rowe, Nicholas: edition of Shakespeare, 3

148

Rowley, Samuel, 42, 49, 57
Roxana (William Alabaster): title page, 3, 4
Rubens: Whitehall ceiling, 87, 96, 99

Samwell, Richard, and family, 34-54 *passim*
Schoenbaum, Samuel: on Bentley, 69; "Shakespeare the Ignoramus," 70; revision of Harbage's *Annals of English Drama 975-1700*, 28
Selden, John: *Historie of Tithes*, 112, 114
Serlio, Sebastiano: *Architettura*, 4
Shakespeare, William: as a mannerist, 120; First Folio, 79; *Antony*, 139, 143; *AYL*, 9, 127, 129; *Com.*, 67, 74; *Cym.*, 10, 13, 76, 77, 79, 87, 93, 99; *Ham.*, 2, 13, 19, 26, 79, 121, 123, 126; *1H4*, 19, 141; *2H4*, 141; *H5*, 68, 74; *H6*, 73; *The true tragedie of Richard Duke of Yorke*, 73, 79; *H8*, 87; *JC*, 10, 79; *Lear*, 9, 87, 121, 123, 128, 139-41; *LLL*, 130; *Mac.*, 13, 67, 77, 87, 99, 123, 143; *MM*, 9; *Mer.*, 129; *MW*, 2, 12; *MND*, 124-25; *Ado.*, 74, 130; *Oth.*, 2, 10, 19; *Per.*, 67, 74, 77, 79; *R2*, 12n; *R3*, 26, 73; *Rom.*, 86, 127, 139, 143; *Shr.*, 130; *Tmp.*, 13, 76, 79, 128; *Tim.*, 7, 15, 23; *Tit.*, 73; *Troi.*, 12, 15, 126; *TN*, 2, 9, 67, 123, 128; *TGV*, 16; *TNK*, 13, 26, 76; *WT*, 12, 76, 77, 79, 86-99
Sheridan, R. B., 125; *The School for Scandal*, 130-31
Shirley, Sir Thomas, 112
Sidney, Sir Philip, 105, 110, 107n; *Apology for Poetry*, 15
Sisson, C. J.: on *Believe as you List*, 72; "The Mythical Sorrows of Shakespeare," 137
Spelman, Sir Henry, 105, 111
Stamm, Rudolf, 140, 141n
Steeves, H. R.: *Learned Societies and English Literary Scholarship*, 107n
Stow, John: *Survey of London*, 35, 103, 105
Strindberg, August, 132
Strype, John: *Life of Parker*, 103
Sypher, Wylie: *Four Stages of Renaissance Style*, 120

Tate, Francis, 107
Theatres: Blackfriars, 5, 8, 15, 16, 20, 23, 32, 33, 67-80 *passim*; Boar's Head, 33-65; Chambers of Rhetoric, 121; Cockpit-in-Court, 2 (drawings), 5; Curtain, 68; Duke's, 64; Fortune, 33, 55, 72, 73, 76; Globe, 1, 5, 8, 17, 32, 33, 67-79 *passim*, 95, 117; Gray's Inn, 67; Hampton Court, 5, 67; Hope, 117; Inns of Court, 15; Middle Temple, 5, 67; Paul's, 15, 16; Phoenix, 8; Red Bull, 8, 33, 73; Rose, 11, 73, 75; St. James, 5; Swan (drawing), 1, 55, 80, (theatre), 33, 38, 117; Theatre, 71, 72, 74; Trinity Hall, 2-3, 4; Whitehall, 5, 67, 74
Torelli, Giacomo, 11
Tynan, Kenneth, 133

Ussher, Bishop, 112, 113

Vega, Lope de, 84

Waiting for Godot (S. Beckett), 134
Walsingham, Thomas: *Historia brevis, Ypodigma Neustriae*, 103
Webster, John: additions to *Malcontent*, 17; *Duchess of Malfi*, 31, 32, 73; *The Famous History of Sir Thomas Wyatt*, 16; *Northward Ho*, 15, 16, 27-28; *Westward Ho*, 14, 15, 16-20, 22-31 *passim*
Wentworth, Anne, 34
Wentworth, Thomas, 34
Wentworth, Lord, 114
Whitehead, A., 123
Whitgift, John, 105
Who's Afraid of Virginia Woolf (Edward Albee), 133
Wickham, Glynne: on "court" plays, 80-81; on Worcester's Men, 76
Wigand, John, 103
Wigand, John, 103
Wilson, Arthur: *History of Great Britain under James I*, 95
The Wits or Sport Upon Sport (frontispiece), 3, 4
Wolfflin, Heinrich: *Principles of Art History*, 120
Woodliffe, Oliver, and family, 34-54 *passim*
Woolf, Virginia, 70, 81